Fargo loosed off three quick shots, hoping that the Murrays were stupid enough to be riding in front of the gang. Jed and the others opened up about that time, and the gang members started firing off their pistols and rifles. Bright muzzle flashes lit up the dark and showed the faces of the men in reddish light.

Someone fired in the direction of the muzzle flash from Fargo's Colt, but Fargo had already flattened himself on the floor of the loft. As he reloaded, he looked over the edge at the fighting that was going on below and saw the vague outlines of black figures striking out with hoes and pitchforks and a scythe or two. He heard the grunting of their efforts and the yells of men being jabbed by a pitchfork or sliced by a scythe. Men were being pulled off their horses now, and it was becoming impossible for Fargo to distinguish between friend and foe. He decided it was time for him to leave the loft, and when a horseman passed beneath him, he dropped over the edge and landed behind the rider.

The horse reared up, and Fargo put his arms around the rider, finding to his surprise that he wasn't behind a horseman at all but a woman. . . .

THE
TRAILSMAN
#260

BLOOD
WEDDING

by

Jon Sharpe

A SIGNET BOOK

SIGNET
Published by New American Library, a division of
Penguin Group (USA) Inc., 375 Hudson Street,
New York, New York 10014, U.S.A.
Penguin Books Ltd, 80 Strand,
London WC2R 0RL, England
Penguin Books Australia Ltd, 250 Camberwell Road,
Camberwell, Victoria 3124, Australia
Penguin Books Canada Ltd, 10 Alcorn Avenue,
Toronto, Ontario, Canada M4V 3B2
Penguin Books (N.Z.) Ltd, Cnr Rosedale and Airborne Roads,
Albany, Auckland 1310, New Zealand

Penguin Books Ltd, Registered Offices:
80 Strand, London WC2R 0RL, England

First published by Signet, an imprint of New American Library,
a division of Penguin Group (USA) Inc.

First Printing, June 2003
10 9 8 7 6 5 4 3 2 1

The first chapter of this book previously appeared in *Wyoming Wolf Pack,*
the two hundred fifty-ninth volume in this series.

 REGISTERED TRADEMARK—MARCA REGISTRADA

Printed in the United States of America

PUBLISHER'S NOTE
This is a work of fiction. Names, characters, places, and incidents either are the
product of the author's imagination or are used fictitiously, and any resemblance
to actual persons, living or dead, events, or locales is entirely coincidental.

The Trailsman

Beginnings . . . they bend the tree and they mark the man. Skye Fargo was born when he was eighteen. Terror was his midwife, vengeance his first cry. Killing spawned Skye Fargo, ruthless, cold-blooded murder. Out of the acrid smoke of gunpowder still hanging in the air, he rose, cried out a promise never forgotten.

The Trailsman they began to call him all across the West: searcher, scout, hunter, the man who could see where others only looked, his skills for hire but not his soul, the man who lived each day to the fullest, yet trailed each tomorrow. Skye Fargo, the Trailsman, the seeker who could take the wildness of a land and the wanting of a woman and make them his own.

Kansas 1859—
The bonds of marriage are meant to last forever;
but when the vows exchanged include revenge,
death may come before "I do."

1

Skye Fargo wasn't fond of weddings. He was a Trailsman, a man given to wandering, sometimes leading other people where they wanted to go, sometimes journeying on his own. He liked the mountains and the sky. He liked being able to see the far horizons, and he liked the feel of a good horse under him. He couldn't quite grasp the idea of a man giving up his freedom to tie himself to one woman and one spot of earth. There was nothing wrong with settling down and having a family for other people, but it wasn't for Fargo.

Sometimes, though, the celebrations leading up to the wedding were all right, especially if there was food, music, dancing, and pretty women. Jedadiah Brand had taken care to provide all those things, and Fargo surely appreciated them.

"This is a mighty fine celebration, Jed," Fargo said as he looked out at the dancers in the big barn.

At one end of the barn, there was a small platform where a fiddler was sawing away, calling the dance at the same time, and Fargo could smell the dust that the couples on the floor were raising as they moved enthusiastically to the fiddler's tune. There were several children there, cutting a rug in improvised dances of their own. Fargo knew men who would ride for two days to go to a good dance, and this was a good one indeed.

There was food, too, on long tables at the end of the barn opposite the fiddler: the smell of freshly baked bread mingled with the smell of the dust, and there was corn on the cob, green beans, yellow crookneck squash, and good

Kansas beef. Fargo had already tried a little of everything, and he planned to eat some more later on.

Some of the women dancers were as pretty as Fargo had seen for a while. Of course, some of them weren't, but that didn't bother Fargo any. He liked women in general, and he was always glad to be around them.

"Hard to believe a man would get married," Fargo said, "with all those beauties around to tempt him."

"I can't be tempted by any but Abby," Jed said. "You know that, Skye."

Abigail, known to all as Abby, was dancing with her father, Lemuel Watkins, a tall man with black hair going gray, wide shoulders, and big hands. Abby didn't look a thing like him. She was small and blond, with very blue eyes and a figure that would make a deacon think twice about his marriage vows. Fargo figured she took after her mother, who had died a few years earlier.

"I can't say as I blame you," Fargo said, "but it didn't use to be that way."

The truth was that when Fargo had known Jed in former days, he had been after women like a bear after honey, pretty much the same as Fargo. Jed had guided a few wagon trains with Fargo, and more than once he had come close to getting himself shot because he couldn't stay away from a pretty woman. All that had changed when he met Abby Watkins. According to Jed, the first time he saw her, he felt like a man who'd been kicked in the head by a stallion, and from that time on he'd never even thought about another woman.

"And you know, Skye," he'd told Fargo, "women were all I used to think about. Even for a while around here, I couldn't keep my hands off of 'em. But I'm a different man now."

He surely was. He'd given up his wandering life, and he was going to be a Kansas farmer. Instead of leading wagon trains out of St. Louis, he was going to let other men, men like Fargo, take the pilgrims out of the plains. He was going to walk behind a mule, plow up the earth, and plant seeds. He was going to feed his chickens and grow his corn and cattle and try to make a living at it. Before long, if everything went the way Jed planned, he would have sons to help him out.

2

Fargo wondered a little about that. Lemuel Watkins had never had sons of his own, but he did have a pretty daughter and a big farm, along with a big barn and a tight-plastered house. Now, because of the daughter, he was getting himself a son to share the work, since Jed and Abby planned to live on the farm with him.

"It will be our farm when he passes on," Jed had explained, so maybe he and Watkins were both getting something out of the deal.

And Jed was getting Abby into the bargain, so Fargo figured it wasn't such a bad trade. Not one that he'd make, but not bad if that was what a man wanted.

"It's going to be a good life, Fargo," Jed said. "Different, that's for sure, and not what I'm used to, but good. With Abby, it would have to be."

"I wish you well," Fargo said, "and now, if you don't mind, I'd like to have a dance with your bride-to-be."

"As long as you're going to stand up for me tomorrow at the wedding, I can't very well refuse you the pleasure of a dance," Jed said. "But I know you from way back, Fargo. Just be sure to keep your hands where they belong and to talk about the weather or the music."

"If I didn't know better, I'd think you didn't trust me."

"I trust you all right, but when a wolf is in among the hens, it pays to be a little extra careful. Lem lost nearly seventy-five hens to wolves last winter, and I don't plan to lose Abby to any wolf, animal or human, not even you."

Fargo laughed. "You're already talking like a farmer, Jed. But you don't have to worry about me. I'd never try anything funny with anybody you cared about. You know that."

"You're right. I do. So go have your dance, and have some fun. Not too much fun, though."

The fiddler's tune was over, and the dancers were taking a breath before he got started again. There were several young men moving in Abby's direction, but Fargo got to her first, and the other men stopped and looked at each other disgustedly for a second or two before moving off to find other partners.

It was clear that they didn't think much of Fargo, who looked different from all of them. They were dressed in their Sunday best, while Fargo was in his buckskins. And while most of them were lean and fit from working their farms, there was something about Fargo's build that suggested he knew how to handle himself in dangerous situations. And that he had, more than once.

Fargo had met Abby earlier, and she greeted him with a slightly worried smile.

"I'm glad you're here, Fargo," she said as they began the dance. "Jed could use a few more friends like you."

There wasn't time to say more, but Fargo knew what she meant. He'd talked to Jed and Lem about it the day before when he'd arrived at the farm. Kansas was in a turmoil because of the slavery issue. The free-staters were moving in and settling down, determined that there would be no slavery there, while the pro-slavery crowd was just as determined that Kansas would enter the union as a slaveholding state. The two groups had come into conflict, and the conflict had eventually become violent, with bloody clashes becoming more and more frequent, particularly in the eastern part of the state where the Watkins farm was located. The territorial government favored slavery and got the help of the United States Army to keep the free-staters under control, but the free-staters formed their own militia to fight back.

To make things worse, outlaw gangs, some of whom had been raiding the countryside for years, took advantage of the situation to increase their pillaging. They robbed and killed whenever and wherever they could while seeing to it that either the free-staters or the pro-slavery group got at least part of the blame for their crimes. It didn't matter to the outlaws who got killed as long as their actions were thought of as patriotic by one side or the other, for the more fighting they could stir up between the two factions, the better it was for them.

Jed didn't want to have anything to do with either side in the slavery fight, and he hated the outlaws. As he'd told Fargo, "All I want to do is settle down and be a farmer. I don't want to have to carry a gun and be looking over my shoulder all the time."

He didn't sound quite convincing, and there was a shifty look in his eyes, as if he might have wanted to say more, but Lem Watkins was with them, and Jed deferred to him.

Lem Watkins felt pretty much as Jed said he did.

"A plague on all their houses," Watkins said. "I've been

a decent, hardworking man all my life. I don't hold with slavery, but my hand fits a plow, not a gun. If people want to fight over who's a slave and who's free, let 'em do it somewhere else. Those other killers all just need hanging, and the sooner the better."

Fargo could understand how Jed and his future father-in-law felt, but he knew things didn't always work themselves out in a peaceful way. A man couldn't always avoid a fight, no matter how much he might want to. Fargo didn't particularly enjoy having to use his Colt, but he had, and more than once. He preferred to settle things without shooting, but one thing he'd learned in his travels was that there were times when you had to let a pistol do the talking. There were too many people who didn't understand any other language. Jed knew that, too, as well as Fargo did, but maybe the idea of becoming a farmer had helped him forget it.

Fargo led Abby through the dance, which was some kind of a variation on the Virginia reel, and they were too busy to talk. When the dance was over, Abby's face was flushed with exertion, and Fargo felt a little warm himself.

"Could we go outside and talk?" Abby asked.

"I'm not sure Jed would like that," Fargo said. "He might get the wrong idea."

Abby's face got even redder. She said, "He knows me better than that."

Fargo gave her a grin. "He knows me, too."

"You men. That's all you ever think about."

"Nope," Fargo said. "But it's one of the things. Sometimes we've got to plan on what to have for supper." This was enough to get a laugh out of her.

"Well, I don't talk about it, not even to Jed. Now, can we please go outside? It's important."

"If you say so."

They walked the length of the barn, and Fargo could feel the eyes of the young men on him. He knew everyone wondered why he and Abby were going outside, and he hoped they didn't get the wrong idea. In spite of his earlier joking, he thought he knew what Abby wanted to talk about, and it had nothing at all to do with sporting around.

Not that he wouldn't have liked to give Abby a tumble. She seemed a little more prim and proper than the women who Fargo usually liked, but that could be just a cover. You could never tell for sure just by looking.

Fargo put his impure thoughts out of his mind. Abby, after all, was marrying Jed, and Fargo was going to stand up with them as best man. He would never betray a friend.

They went out through the big barn doors, and Abby said, "We don't have to go far. Nobody's going to follow us."

Fargo wasn't too sure of that. Jed might take a notion to see what was going on, though Fargo hoped he wouldn't.

The moon hung big and bright in the night sky, which was dotted with high, icy stars. There was a light breeze that fluttered through the cornfields beyond the barn.

"What did you want to talk about?" Fargo asked.

Abby looked off into the dark fields. "I said that Jed could use a few friends like you. Did you know what I meant?"

"There's been some trouble around here, so I heard."

"Trouble? Is that what you call it?"

"Can't think of a better word," Fargo said.

"Well, it's worse than trouble. People are being killed and robbed every day. Some of them have had their houses burned."

Fargo wanted to ask what that had to do with him, but he was afraid he already knew the answer.

"Jed and your father told me they didn't have anything to do with the trouble around here."

"I'm sure they did. As far as my father goes, that's true. It's not so true for Jed. He was just saying what my father wanted to hear."

Fargo had been afraid that might be the case. Jed's evident lack of conviction when they'd been discussing it had made him wonder. Jed hadn't forgotten how people were, after all.

"So he's been getting mixed up in things, has he?" Fargo said.

"You know him. Are you surprised?"

Fargo grinned. "Not much. Which side is he taking? Is he for a Free State or a slaveholding one?"

"Free, but that's not the real problem around here."

"What is, then?" Fargo asked.

"The Murray gang, that's what. Have you heard of them?"

6

Fargo had heard of them, all right. You didn't have to be where you got a newspaper every day to hear about the Murrays. Father, son, and daughter had joined together with a bunch of ragtag outlaws who killed as much for the fun of it as for the profit they might find.

"What does Jed have to do with the Murrays?" Fargo asked.

"He's spoken out against them. He's even tried to talk some of the farmers around here into forming a vigilance group to fight them."

"Does your father know about this?"

"Jed doesn't talk about it around him, but he hasn't made a secret of the way he feels when he talks in town."

"As long as Lem isn't around."

"That's right. Jed doesn't want him to get upset."

"Why would he do that?"

"Because he knows how Murray is. Most people who talk against him get their houses and crops burned. If they're lucky."

"What if they're not lucky?"

"Then they get killed."

"I can see why Lem doesn't want to get mixed up in it. But Jed has always had a mind of his own."

"He has more responsibilities now," Abby said.

If Fargo was peeved by her casual assumption that men like him had no responsibilities, he didn't show it. After all, it wasn't her fault that she didn't know how things were out on the trail or in the settlements farther out west. There were responsibilities aplenty for anyone who'd take them, and Jed had never been shy about doing it. He wasn't shying away now, either, to hear Abby tell it.

"So you want Jed to forget about Murray and stick to his farming," Fargo said.

Abby smiled. She had a nice smile that made little dimples appear in both cheeks.

"That's right," she said. "I want him to. But do you think he will?"

"Not likely."

"You do know him, don't you? But I haven't told you everything."

No wonder Jed had looked so shifty, Fargo thought. He asked what else Abby had to tell him about.

7

"Angel Murray," Abby said. "She and Jed used to be . . . friends."

Angel was the daughter of Peter Murray, the gang leader, and the sister of Paul, Peter's son and second in command. Fargo didn't have to ask how Angel and Jed had known each other. If Angel was as pretty as the stories had it, Jed wouldn't have asked her much about her family's habits when he first met her.

"I guess they were pretty good friends," Fargo said.

The look in Jed's eyes when they'd discussed the outlaw gangs was pretty much explained now, and Fargo figured that there had been other women as well, knowing Jed, even though he was interested only in Abby now.

"Yes, they were good friends," Abby said. "If that's what you want to call it. But now they're not. She hates Jed because he quit seeing her when he found out about what she and her family did. And that's why he needs a friend like you. Most of the people in there . . ." Abby paused and looked back at the barn. "Well, they're good people. Like my father. He'd do anything for me, or for his neighbors. But they think they can stay out of a fight if they just look the other way. It doesn't work like that."

Fargo thought maybe he'd underestimated her. She wasn't as naive as she'd sounded only a few seconds before.

"So," she went on, "I was hoping you could stay around for a while. We could use a good hand around here."

"I'm not much good at farming," Fargo told her.

"I wasn't thinking about farming."

"I was afraid of that," Fargo said. "You think Jed's in danger, then."

"I think we all are. You said you knew about the Murrays."

"Revenge," Fargo said. "That's what they claim causes them to be the way they are."

"That's right. Their story is that they've been done wrong by everybody in the territory, and all they're doing now is getting a little of their own back."

"By killing and burning and stealing," Fargo said.

"Any way they can. That's what they say. I think they just do it because they like it."

Fargo thought the same thing, but he was surprised that Abby did. She was seeming less innocent by the minute.

"You didn't happen to invite them to the wedding, I guess."

"No, of course not. Why do you ask?"

"Because I think they might be on the way," Fargo said.

2

Fargo could hear the music coming from the barn, the clucking of the chickens on their roosts, the sound of the wind in the cornstalks. Those were the things that most people could have heard, if they'd listened for them. But Fargo had spent most of his life listening for things that not just anyone could hear, and now he heard the distant sound of hoofbeats, headed in the direction of the farm.

"You think the Murrays are coming here?" Abby said.

"It might not be the Murrays," Fargo said, "but it's a lot of riders. I think we should get back to the barn."

Abby didn't waste any time questioning him further, another point in her favor. She gathered her skirts and ran for the big open doors of the barn.

She had a head start, but Fargo, with his long, loping strides got there just a little ahead of her. He started swinging the tall doors shut while Abby ran to stand beside the fiddler and shout a warning.

"The Murrays are coming!"

She had to yell it twice before anybody paid her any attention. The second time, the fiddler stopped playing, his lively song ending on a squealing note that trailed off into nothing. The dancers stopped and turned to the stage.

"The Murrays are coming," Abby said again into the silence that had settled in the barn.

The only other sound was the squealing of door hinges, and Fargo thought he and Abby were going to look pretty foolish if the riders passed the farm by or if they were only more guests, arriving late to the dance.

"What are we going to do?" somebody called out.

Fargo hadn't thought much about that, but then he realized that the people in the barn were farmers. They wore pistols. They didn't carry rifles. Of all the men there, only he and a couple of others, including Jed, had weapons. And they weren't carrying them. They'd put them aside when the dance started.

"Get your guns," Fargo said. "And then see if you can block the door with something."

Barn doors weren't made to be barred from the inside, and there was nothing more needed than a gentle push to open them. The Murray gang could ride right on in.

Fargo went over to the wall where he'd hung his gun belt on a nail. He took the belt down and buckled it on while Jed and several other men started stacking grain sacks against the doors. Fargo knew the bags wouldn't stop anyone for very long. He looked around the barn for more weapons. There were a few tools, but that was all.

"Pitchforks in the loft," Lem said at his side. "I got a shotgun in the house."

"Too late for the shotgun," Fargo said. "Grab a hoe."

He smelled the dry hay as he started up the ladder to the high loft that ran half the length of the barn. There were no lanterns hanging up there, but Fargo thought how easily the whole barn could go up.

"Put out the lanterns," he called.

It wouldn't matter if the barn were in darkness. In fact, it would make things better. There was no danger of any of Jed's guests shooting each other, since they weren't armed, and the darkness would make it harder for the gang to find targets.

He reached the loft and tossed down a couple of pitchforks with long, curving tines.

"Don't hit anyone who's not on a horse," he said.

Lem caught a pitchfork and said, "Get those lanterns out, like he told us."

Several of the young men ran around the barn and doused the lights as the thudding of hoofbeats shook the ground outside the door.

There was one lantern left on, and long shadows danced around the barn walls before it was extinguished. In the sudden darkness there was gunfire from outside, and bullets smacked into the hard wood of the barn doors.

No doubt about it, Fargo thought, it was the Murray gang, all right.

There were only a few shots and then more silence. Fargo could hear the people in the barn moving around as they sought through the darkness for a place to hide. One of the younger children started crying, but the noise was cut off as someone covered his mouth. Fargo didn't blame him for crying. There wouldn't be much use in hiding if the Murrays got inside. People were going to die, and most of them would be farmers, not gang members.

Fargo could hear yelling outside, and then the barn doors began to slide slowly back into the barn. Fargo pulled the big Colt from its holster and got ready. The only advantage he and the other couple of armed men had was that they were in almost total darkness, whereas the Murrays would be silhouetted against the faint light from the moon and stars. Fargo hoped Jed had enough sense to hold his fire until more of the gang was bunched in the doorway.

Fargo needn't have worried. Jed had always been cool even in a tight spot, and apparently the few other men with guns knew what to do.

The doors opened wider, and when they did, riders started to plunge through them. There were fifteen or twenty of them, all whooping and yelling and spurring up their mounts. Fargo couldn't tell which one was Angel, not that it mattered. She'd have to take her chances with the rest of them.

Fargo loosed off three quick shots, hoping that the Murrays were stupid enough to be riding in front of the gang. He didn't think that would be the case, but he was gratified to see three dark figures pitch backward off their horses.

Jed and the others opened up about that time, and the gang members started firing off their pistols and rifles. The bright muzzle flashes lit up the dark and showed the faces of the men in reddish light. Fargo fired again, but by then the Murrays were all inside and it wasn't easy to pick them off without endangering everyone else.

Someone fired in the direction of the muzzle flash from Fargo's Colt, but Fargo had already flattened himself on the floor of the loft. As he reloaded, he looked over the edge at the fighting that was going on below and saw the vague outlines of black figures striking out with hoes and pitchforks and a scythe or two. He heard the grunting of their efforts and the yells of men being jabbed by a pitchfork or sliced by

12

a scythe. Men were being pulled off their horses now, and it was becoming impossible for Fargo to distinguish between friend and foe. He decided it was time for him to leave the loft, and when a horseman passed beneath him, he dropped over the edge and landed behind the rider.

The horse reared up, and Fargo put his arm around the rider, finding to his surprise that he wasn't behind a horseman at all but a woman. His hands held her soft, pillowy breasts, but he didn't have time to enjoy the experience. She snapped her head back in an attempt to catch him sharply on the point of the chin. He might have fallen if he hadn't been ready for some such trick, and he had moved his head far enough to the side so that he caught only a glancing blow. He twisted her roughly and threw her from the horse. He wasn't worried about where she landed or about whether she was under the horse's hoofs. He pulled his pistol and looked around for other riders.

He saw muzzle shots as pistols were fired, but he didn't know who was doing the shooting now, so he didn't try firing any shots in the direction of the flares. He saw one big horse wheeling in the middle of the barn, and the dark rider was yelling something that Fargo couldn't quite understand. He pointed his Colt in that direction, but before he could pull the trigger, someone grabbed his left leg and gave a hard yank, pulling him from the saddle.

Fargo landed hard on his back. Someone kicked him in the head, and his finger tightened on the trigger of the Colt, sending a wild shot along the dirt floor of the barn. Fargo's head throbbed, and there was dirt in his eyes. He expected that his attacker would shoot him, or at least kick him again, but it didn't happen. He pawed dirt from his eyes and saw that the woman he'd pulled from the horse was mounting it again, and then the Murray gang was helling it out the barn, yelling and waving their hats as if they'd won some kind of victory.

Fargo had to roll aside to keep from being trampled. The farmers fired a few shots after the riders, and then it was quiet in the barn except for some moans from the wounded and the crying of frightened children. The air was filled with acrid smoke from the pistol shots.

"Get those lanterns lit," Lemuel Watkins called out, and after a few seconds someone followed his orders.

Fargo stood up, his knees a little shaky, and touched a hand to his head. There was no blood, but a lump was forming just above his right temple. He holstered his Colt and looked around the barn.

There were men standing with their hands to bloodied shoulders and heads, at least one woman had been hit in the arm. As far as Fargo could see, none of the children had been hurt. Several horses were milling around, and Lemuel gave orders to get them under control. They had belonged to dead outlaws, of whom Fargo saw at least five.

Over to one side of the barn, a man lay face down in the dirt, the back of his head blown off. Fargo felt his insides go hollow. Even from where he stood he could tell that the dead man was Jed Brand.

Fargo and Lemuel got Jed into the house and laid him out on the kitchen table. One of the women was with Abby in another room. Abby had cried wildly at first, but when Fargo had last seen her, she had been icily calm.

Lemuel looked down at Jed's body and shook his head.

"Not much good you can say about a thing like this. We got more of them than they got of us, but I do hate it that they got Jed. He was a fine young man, and he'd have made a good husband for Abby."

"He was the one they were after," Fargo said, though something about the way things had happened bothered him. It seemed to him that there was more to it than met the eye, but he couldn't quite figure out what it was. "Abby told me he spoke out against them."

"Yeah," Lemuel said. "He thought I didn't know about it, but I did. I didn't like it because I knew what could happen. I'm not much of a man to go looking for a fight. I thought that if we'd leave the Murray gang alone, they'd leave us alone."

"People like that don't leave anybody alone."

"I guess I know that now. Did Abby tell you that Angel Murray was sweet on Jed at one time?"

"She told me. I think I met Angel tonight."

"Met her? How could you do that?"

"We had a little tussle," Fargo said. "You wouldn't say that we got properly introduced."

"She'd be the one that shot him," Lemuel said. He ran

his fingers through his gray hair. "She's a beauty, but she's mean as a snake."

"I don't think she shot him. She was too busy. I threw her off her horse, and then she pulled me off it."

"She could've shot him before all that. Those Murrays don't like to be slighted. They always get back at whoever does it."

"So I've heard."

"You say that like you've had a little experience."

"I have," Fargo told him. "I'd better go to the barn and help with those bodies."

"Hell, we oughta just put 'em in a pile and burn 'em. Sons of bitches."

Fargo knew the old man didn't really mean it, though he wouldn't have blamed him if he did.

"You go on," Lem said. "I'll go see how Abby is doing."

He left the kitchen and Fargo looked down at Jed's body, which lay under a sheet on the wooden table.

"You have to get them," Abby said at his back.

Fargo turned slowly. He said, "I thought your father had gone to see about you."

"I don't need anybody to see about me. I sent Sue Ballew home, and I told my father to go on to bed. You're the one I want to talk to. You're the one who knows what to do when something like this happens."

"What makes you think that?" Fargo asked.

"The way you look. The things Jed told me about you. He said you were a man who knew a thing or two about revenge."

Fargo thought about it. He'd gone on the vengeance trail long ago, family business as it was. But it hadn't been any good, not in the long run. His life was no longer consumed by a need for revenge. He'd gone past that a long time ago.

"A man who goes looking for revenge usually finds a lot of things he wishes he hadn't," Fargo said.

"That may be so," Abby said, "but don't bother telling it to the Murrays. Do you think they'll forget what happened tonight?"

"They did what they came to do."

"But they didn't get an even exchange. Jed's dead, but so are four of the gang members. And one of them is Paul Murray."

"The father?" Fargo asked.

"No, the son. The father's name is Peter. It would have been better if he'd been killed because they say Paul wasn't quite as crazy as his old man. And his sister. They'll come after us again, and after everybody who was at that dance."

"How will they find out?"

"They already know. You can count on that. They know everything that goes on around here."

Fargo wasn't surprised to hear it. There was already plenty of talk in and around small communities. You didn't have to be too clever to pick up any information you wanted.

"The Murrays operate out of this area?" he asked.

"Nobody knows just where they stay. I don't think they ever stay in one place for long. They've robbed and killed all over the state. You have to do something about them."

Fargo started to tell her that it wasn't his job. He had other places to go and other things to do. But for some reason he kept his mouth shut. Finally he said, "I'll think it over. Right now, I have to go to the barn."

"Jed was your friend," Abby said, as if that settled everything, and in a way it did. But Fargo wasn't ready to tell her that.

"I'll talk to you tomorrow," he said.

3

Many of the people who had come to the dance had gone on back home, but there were still several men and a few women in the barn. They had pulled the bodies of the dead outlaws to the side and raked dirt over the blood on the floor. The outlaws' weapons were stacked on the table with the food that would now serve for a funeral meal. Most of the men were standing around in a little knot, talking in low voices. The women were standing by the table, not saying much of anything to anybody.

"We caught most of the horses," a tall, gangly man said to Fargo. "Got 'em over to the little corral, but that won't hold 'em. It's not meant for more than a couple of mules. Name's Frank Conner, by the way."

"Mine's Fargo."

"Yeah. Jed's friend from out west. I heard about you. I figger you're more or less in charge tonight, since Lem's not here and Jed's dead."

Fargo didn't want to be in charge, but he didn't see any way out of it. He said, "We need to see about getting those bodies buried tonight. No sense leaving them to ripen till morning."

He thought about Jed in the kitchen. Well, Jed would keep.

"Where we gonna bury 'em?" Conner asked. "I don't know that they're worth hauling to the cemetery, and it's certain and sure nobody wants 'em in the churchyard."

Fargo had looked the Watkins place over when he arrived the day before, and he knew it was located on a little creek. There was some marshy land down by the creek that wasn't fit for farming, and the digging would be easy enough. He told Conner to take the bodies there, and asked if there were any other men who could stay and help with the work.

"I'll help," someone said at Fargo's shoulder.

He turned to see a woman almost as tall as he was. She was wide through the shoulders and narrow at the waist, but she flared out at the hips. She wasn't wearing a dress as the other women had been. She had on a pair of heavy work boots, a cotton shirt, and thick denim pants.

"I'm Molly," she said in a voice almost as deep as a man's. "Alice, really, but everybody calls me Molly. Molly Doyle. And I can dig as long and deep as any man here."

As if to prove it, she stuck out her hand for Fargo to shake. It was as big as his own, and callused hard as bone by a lifetime of labor.

"Got my own place close by here," Molly said. "It's small, and I pretty much run it by myself, but I can outwork any man in this barn."

"There's some might question that," Conner said, and Molly gave him a hard look. "Not that I'd be one of them. I know better than to say a thing like that. I'll tell you, Fargo, Molly could probably whip half the men in here."

"Half, hell," Molly said. "All of 'em."

"I won't argue that with you either," Conner told her. "I know it's rough on you about Jed, and I'm sorry for that."

"Jed never gave a rat's ass for me, and you know it, Frank Conner. Now, let's get busy and get those bodies out of here."

"I'll hitch Lem's mules to his wagon, and we can pile 'em on there," Conner said. "Be a lot easier than dragging them."

"Good idea," Fargo said, and Conner walked away.

"He's one who won't be all that sorry that Jed got killed," Molly said when Conner was out of earshot.

"Why's that?" Fargo asked.

" 'Cause he was sweet on Abby before Jed moved in on him. He thought he was the one who'd be marrying her and getting himself set up with this farm."

"I thought he already had a farm."

"He does, but it's nothing to speak of. He's not much of a worker, and he doesn't make good crops. Not much of a builder, either. You could put his house and barn inside this place here and still have room for a few cows and mules."

"Maybe he just had an eye for a pretty woman."

Molly considered that. "Could be. There were a couple of others who had the same idea he did, and one of 'em was even married."

Fargo didn't care to hear about Abby's suitors right at the moment. He said, "Judging from what Conner said, I'd guess you were sweet on Jed."

"You'd be right about that, for all the good it ever did me. I'm not a delicate little flower like Abby, and I guess Jed didn't want a woman who could work just as hard and as long as he could. He wanted somebody he could sit in a parlor and look pretty." Molly grinned. "Not a damned thing wrong with that. It's just not my style, as you can see."

She wasn't exactly pretty, Fargo thought, but she wasn't ugly, either. She had a good smile, and while she was big, covering up her body in men's clothes, he could see the outlines of generous curves.

"Maybe Jed didn't know what he was missing," Fargo said.

Molly's smile widened, and she said, "You got that right, Fargo, but then most men are afraid of a big woman. Maybe you're not."

"Maybe," Fargo said.

At that point Conner came back into the barn, leading a couple of lop-eared mules hitched to a wagon. He led the mules over to where the bodies lay and looked around for help.

Fargo looked at Molly. "I guess we'd better help him load them."

"Doesn't look like anybody else is rushing to do it. Let's go."

"I'll get us some help," Molly said. "Johnson, Talley, get over here. You, too, Wesley."

At the sound of her yell, three men detached themselves from the group and looked at her.

"We're gonna take care of the bodies," Molly said. "Come on and make yourselves useful."

If the men were bothered that a woman was ordering them around, they didn't show it. Fargo and Molly walked over to the bodies where Conner was already standing, and the three men joined them there. Nobody said anything, and Fargo bent over to grab a man's body by the shoulders.

"Somebody get his legs," Fargo said, and Molly grabbed his ankles. They swung the body once and pitched it in the wagon bed.

A short man with a red face and a thick neck bent over the next body, took a good look at the face, and said, "Shit."

"That's no way to talk in front of a lady, Alf Wesley," Molly said.

"I don't see no ladies real close by here, Molly," Wesley said. "What I do see is trouble. How about it, Talley?"

Talley, who had a thin face with its features all squashed together in the middle of it, said, "I think you're probably right, Alf. Goddamn, how was anybody to know? I wish to hell I'd stayed home tonight."

"You came for the same reason I did," Wesley told him. "You wanted one last sniff of Abby before she got married. And now that she ain't getting married, maybe both of us still have a chance."

"That's a terrible thing to say," the third man told them.

"You can't fool us, Rip Johnson," Talley said, squinting his close-set eyes. "You might be a married man, but you've been sniffing around Abby as long as I can remember, hoping to get you a little piece on the side."

Fargo looked at Molly. Far from being offended by the rough talk, she seemed to be enjoying herself. As for the men, they seemed to think she was one of them. Fargo knew they would never have talked that way in front of somebody they considered a proper lady.

Conner was the only one who seemed embarrassed. He said, "There's no call for that kind of talk, fellas. Besides, you're getting off the subject. What is it that's going to cause so much trouble for us?"

"Hell," Wesley said. "Can't you see it for yourself?"

"If I could, I wouldn't have asked you."

"Well, take a better look. Who do you think that is lying there."

Conner looked down at the body. The dead face stared back at him with wide-open eyes. It was a young face, with hardly a trace of a beard, but the eyes were hard, as if even in life they had been cold as the moon on a winter night.

"Don't know him," Conner said, looking back at Wesley.

"Well, I sure as hell do, and so does everybody else standing here." He looked at Fargo. "Except maybe you, stranger. What did you say your name was?"

Fargo hadn't mentioned his name, and he didn't remember having met Wesley when he'd been introduced around by Jed earlier in the evening. He didn't go into that, however. He just said, "My name's Fargo."

"You know who this is, Fargo?"

"No, I can't say that I do. Like you said, I'm a stranger around here. Who is it?"

"It's Paul Murray, that's who it is. Peter Murray's son."

"Shit," Conner said.

"Right," Wesley. "That's what I said. 'Shit.' Which is just exactly what's going to come down on us from now on. Pete Murray will never let this go by. He won't know who did it, so he won't know who to kill. It could have been anybody in here that had a gun. Not that it'll make any difference to Pete. He'll just take it out on everybody who was here tonight. We might all be better off if we just packed our duds and cleared off our land right now."

"We've all got too much time and money and sweat invested to do that," Conner said.

"Won't any of that matter if we're dead," Wesley told him.

"Anyhow, I didn't shoot him," Conner said. "I don't even have a pistol."

"You see that pile of weapons over on that table?" Molly asked, pointing toward them.

"Sure, I see 'em. I'm not blind." Conner shrugged. "But they don't have anything to do with me. Those all belonged to the Murray gang."

"And we picked 'em up and put 'em on the table," Johnson said. "So what?"

"You might have picked them up and put them there," Molly said, "but that doesn't mean somebody else didn't pick one up first, use it, and throw it back down. So you can't weasel out of it by saying you didn't have a pistol."

"Dammit, I wasn't trying to weasel out of anything."

"It's not doing us any good to argue about things like

that," Talley said. "Wesley's right. It doesn't matter who killed Murray's son. We're all going to pay for it."

"Maybe we could do something about it," Molly said.

"What would that be?" Talley asked.

"We could go get Murray before he gets us."

"You're sounding just like Jed now," Conner said. "It won't do you any good. You can't impress a dead man."

Molly's face reddened. "I'm not trying to impress anybody. I'm just making sense."

"Right," Wesley said. "The same way Jed made sense, and you see where it got him. Laid out dead as a hammer."

There was still something bothering Fargo about Jed's death, but he couldn't quite figure out what it was. He said, "Where does the Murray gang hide out?"

"They don't have to hide," Molly said, giving Wesley a scornful look. "Everybody's afraid of 'em, so they can walk right down the streets of town without worrying about a thing. Makes it right handy when they want to rob a bank."

"Nothing wrong with wanting to stay alive," Wesley said. "I don't think I'd like being dead one bit."

"You're probably right, considering where you'd be," Molly said. "Might hot there, so I've heard."

Wesley drew himself up to his full height, which put his head on about the level of Molly's shoulders.

"If you weren't a woman, I'd have to bust you for having such a smart mouth."

"You could go ahead and give it a try," Molly said. "And we could see what would happen."

Fargo grinned. "This isn't getting those bodies buried. Let's get them out of here and down to the river bottom."

Wesley grumbled a little, but they loaded the other bodies into the wagon. They found some shovels and put them into the wagon as well, and Conner drove out of the barn while the others sat in the rear with the bodies, except for Molly, who was riding beside him.

The night had gotten a bit cooler, but the air had become still, and Fargo heard the chickens clucking in their sleep. The wagon bounced along a little rutted track through the cornfield and down toward the creek. There were some scraggly trees growing in the marshy ground, a few box elders and cottonwoods. A hoot owl called out from one of the higher branches.

22

The digging was as easy as Fargo had figured, and they were able to dig deep without too much trouble. Between the moon and a lantern that hung from a limb, they had enough light to work by. When the bodies were covered over, Conner suggested that they should mark the graves some way.

"It seems like the respectful thing to do," he said.

"I don't have any respect for these varmints," Molly said.

"I'll tell you what worries me," Wesley said, "and it's not grave markers. It's whether Pete Murray's gonna let his boy lie in an unmarked grave on some sodbuster's farm."

"What choice does he have?" Talley asked. "Besides, when you're dead, you're dead. Where you're lying doesn't matter."

"It might matter to Murray," Wesley said.

"Too bad, then," Molly said. "He's buried already. And that's another good reason not to put any markers up. No need to let Murray know where he is. If he knew, he might come after him."

"Might come anyway," Wesley said. "Might be better if finding him was easy."

Molly threw the shovel she'd used into the wagon. It bounced off the bed and clattered against the side.

"If Murray comes," she said, "Fargo can take care of him. Isn't that right, Fargo."

"I don't even know that I'll be around," Fargo said.

"Oh, you'll be here, all right," Molly said, as if she knew something he didn't. "And if you need any help and these 'men' won't side with you, you just let me know. You can count on me."

"That's nice to know," Fargo said, and they all got in the wagon and rode back to the barn.

4

After everyone had finally gone home, Fargo went back to the Watkins house. He had slept in the spare room the previous night, but he didn't want to disturb anyone now. He could sleep just as well in the barn or outside. He'd spent many a night in less pleasant circumstances.

But there was lantern light shining through a window in the house, and Fargo was curious. He thought that Abby and her father might be talking about Jed's funeral, so he decided to join them.

Fargo went inside the house and heard talking from the kitchen. Fargo walked to the room and looked through the door. Lem hadn't gone to bed after all. He was sitting there not far from the table where Jed's body lay covered with a sheet, and there were two other men with him. Fargo recognized them, having met them before the dance. They were Cass Ellis and Bob Tabor, two of Lem's friends. Ellis was holding a bottle of whiskey, and it was evident from their red faces that they'd been passing it around.

"Come on in, Fargo," Lem said. "We're just sitting up with the body. You want a drink?"

"Might as well," Fargo said.

Ellis extended his arm, and Fargo took the bottle. He took a swallow, and tears came to his eyes. He wiped his mouth with the back of his hand and passed the bottle back to Ellis.

"A little raw, ain't it?" Ellis said. "But it's not so bad once you get used to it."

Fargo nodded and looked at the sheet-covered body on the table. He knew that sitting up was the custom in some parts of the country. He didn't know the reason for it, unless there were places where you had to keep the animals away. There were no animals likely to get into the Watkins' kitchen, so maybe it was just a matter of respect.

"We washed him while you were gone," Lem said. "Dressed him nice and put wet soda cloths on his face and hands. They'll keep his color looking natural. Couldn't do much with that wound, though."

Fargo thought about the wound. He wanted to take another look at it, so he walked to the table and lifted the sheet. Jed's head, what was left of it, was supported on a stained pillow. There was another cloth over Jed's face. Fargo lifted that one off, too.

It appeared to Fargo that the bullet had entered the back of Jed's head and pretty much removed it, though Jed's face was hardly altered. Fargo replaced the cloth and lowered the sheet.

"Gonna bury him tomorrow," Tabor said. He had pale blue eyes and a fringe of white hair around his bald head. "Cass here will make him a good strong coffin in the morning, and we'll bury him in the churchyard in the afternoon. Put him in a real grave, six foot long, six foot deep and four foot wide, not like the ones you dug down in the river bottom."

Fargo didn't think Tabor really knew what kind of graves had been dug for the outlaws, but he was right. Nobody had paid much attention to doing it right. The graves were deep enough to keep animals off the bodies, and that was about all.

"Jed was a fine fella," Ellis said, flexing the fingers of his big hands. "We'll put him facin' the east, all right and proper, the way it should be. Him and Abby would've made a fine couple, Lem. You'd have had some good-lookin' grandchildren, for certain and sure."

Lem didn't reply. Instead he reached out his hand, and Ellis passed him the bottle.

"How's Abby taking it?" Fargo asked.

Lem drank from the bottle. When he could talk again, he said, "About as well as you could expect. She's trying to get some sleep, but I don't know if she'll manage it. You might as well have a try, too. We'll stay here all night, but there's no need for you to do it."

Fargo had thought of offering, but he was glad to be

25

relieved of the responsibility. He'd liked and respected Jed, but now that his friend was dead, he didn't see the need in losing sleep over the matter. He'd do what he could to see that Jed's killer was brought to justice, however. He owed him that much.

"I think I'll go on to bed, then," Fargo said. "Abby asked me earlier if I'd stay around for a few days and help out around the place, and I might be doing that."

"That's mighty kind of you," Lem said. "We could use some help around here, now that Jed's gone."

"She's not worried so much about help as she is about what the Murray gang might do."

"They've killed Jed," Tabor said. "What else could they want around here?"

"More revenge," Fargo told him. "It looks like somebody killed Paul Murray tonight."

"Shit," Ellis said.

"That seems to be pretty much the general opinion," Fargo said.

"Murray'll come after his boy," Tabor said. "He won't want him lying buried in some marsh with no marker. What're you gonna do, Lem?"

"Bury Jed," Lem said. "Then we'll see."

"Murray'll burn your house and barn," Ellis said. "Kill you if he gets the chance."

"We'll just have to see that he doesn't get the chance," Fargo said. "That's one reason I'm staying around."

"What's the other reason?" Lem asked.

"To find out who killed Jed."

"Hell, we all know who did it. It was Murray's gang."

"I'm not so sure about that," Fargo said.

Fargo had had a rough night. First there had been the fighting and then the grave digging. It was well after midnight, and he was bone tired when he lay down on the feather bed to try to get some sleep. He sank into the mattress and was just about to drift off when he heard soft footsteps outside his door, which then slowly swung open.

Fargo looked over in that direction and saw Abby's dark silhouette outlined by the faint lantern light from the kitchen. She entered the room and closed the door behind her.

"Fargo?" she said. "Are you sleeping?"

"Well, I was trying. But I hadn't quite made it yet."

"I didn't mean to bother you, but I wanted to talk a minute. If you don't mind."

Fargo sighed, but not loud enough for her to hear him. She probably needed to talk about Jed, and he could understand that.

"I don't mind," he said. "Let me get up and light the lantern."

It was quite dark in the room, which had only a small window through which the chalky moon shone faintly.

"We don't need the lantern," Abby said. "I'll just sit over here in the chair."

There was a hard-backed wooden chair near the washstand, and Fargo watched as Abby walked over and sat down. He couldn't see her very well, but her blond hair shone palely in the dim light. Fargo couldn't think of anything to say that would soothe her, so he just lay in the bed and waited for her to have her say.

After a few seconds she said, "I guess you think I need to talk about Jed."

"I don't blame you," Fargo said. "You must want to know a little about him, maybe, things a man wouldn't tell you himself. He was a good man, and a brave one. There was a time once when we were on the trail together . . ."

"I didn't come here for that. I didn't really need to talk. That was just an excuse."

If she hadn't come to hear about Jed, there must be something else that was worrying her, Fargo thought, and then he remembered that he hadn't told her for sure that he'd stay around for a while.

"I've decided to stay here for a few days if that's what you came to find out," he said. He didn't mention his suspicions about Jed's death.

"Good. I was hoping you'd stay. But that's not why I came, either."

Fargo couldn't think of anything else left unsettled between them, so he said, "Why did you come, then?"

"I don't want to say."

Fargo thought, not for the first time, and, he was sure, not for the last, that he would never understand women. He liked them. He enjoyed their company, and over the years he had enjoyed the company of more of them than he could count without using a paper and pencil to keep track. But he could never figure out how their minds worked. Abby had come to his room for a reason, but now that she was there, she wouldn't tell him what it was. He wasn't surprised. A man would have come right out and said what it was that he wanted, but a woman wouldn't always do that. Sometimes she had to be coaxed.

"You can go ahead and tell me," Fargo said. If it's a secret, I can keep one about as well as anybody I know."

"That's right. It's a secret. Nobody must ever know."

"Except me."

"Except you. And me, of course. We'll both know."

Her voice wasn't quite right. It had a skittish, trembly quality to it that Fargo hadn't heard before.

"Are you afraid of something?" he asked.

"Just of myself."

Fargo didn't know what she meant by that, and he didn't ask. He wasn't sure she could explain even if she tried. But she surprised him.

"I'm afraid of myself because of what I want," she said.

"We all want things. Nothing to be afraid of there."

"You don't understand, do you?"

She was right about that. Fargo couldn't figure it out, though he was beginning to get a pretty good idea. However, he didn't want to tell her what it was. If she wanted what he thought, she was going to have to say it herself.

"You'll have to tell me," he said.

Instead of explaining, Abby got up out of the chair and came to stand by the bed. Fargo's eyes had gotten used to the faint light in the room, and he could see that she was wearing a flimsy cotton gown that came down below her ankles. She bent over, grabbed the bottom of the gown, pulled it straight up over her head, and tossed it in the general direction of the chair she'd been sitting in. Now she was wearing nothing at all.

"Now do you know what I want?" she asked.

Fargo didn't say anything, and he wasn't surprised. Her desire was a natural reaction to what had happened, he figured. Jed had been killed, and Abby was still alive. But maybe she needed to prove it to herself.

"You think I'm terrible, don't you," she said.

It wasn't a question, and Fargo continued to keep quiet. The next thing he knew, Abby had crawled under the thin sheet that covered him. Her hip and shoulder touched him. They were hot as a smithy's fire.

"I don't care if you do think I'm terrible," she said. "I need you, and I need you now."

Fargo could have played the noble, grieving friend and shoved her out of the bed. But he didn't. He understood her need, and he felt something a little like it himself. He didn't think Jed would mind. Oh, if he'd been alive, he'd have minded. He'd have fought Fargo with his fists or with pistols or with whatever came to hand. But he wasn't alive, and Fargo was. So was Abby. Fargo pulled her to him.

"Oh," she said, feeling his stiff rod as the long length of it pressed against her stomach. "You don't wear anything to sleep in."

"Just a waste, when you're in a soft bed," Fargo said.

And the bed *was* soft. It was so soft that it seemed about to swallow them up, and in doing so it forced them even closer together. Abby's body was feverishly hot, and she hugged Fargo to her, rubbing her belly against his stiffness.

"That's what I need," she said. "I need it now, Fargo. I don't think I can wait."

Fargo rolled over on his back, pulling her on top of him. She was so much smaller than he that he hardly felt her weight.

"I won't break," she said, seeming to know what he was thinking. "Please. Help me."

Fargo was willing. He took her hips in his hands and lifted her, then settled her against the tip of his throbbing erection. He could feel the crisp hairs of her sex, and she rubbed herself vigorously against him. She was slick and hot and ready, and Fargo held her still long enough to locate the stop he was looking for. Then he slid her down onto his rock-hard pole and pinned her there for a moment.

"Ah," she said. "Ah, ah, ah."

She tried to begin wiggling, but eager as she was, Fargo wasn't ready to turn her loose, and not just because he enjoyed having his penis encased by her honeyed heat. He said, "Your father and a couple of his friends are sitting up in the kitchen."

"Ah. I, ah, know. It doesn't matter. Please."

"We might make noise."

"They, ah, they'll be drunk by, ah, now. Please, Fargo. Please. I can't wait."

Fargo hoped she was right about the men being drunk. He didn't want Lem to catch him with Abby. Lem might get the idea that Fargo was being disrespectful of the dead.

But it was really too late to worry about that. Abby was rubbing her breasts against him, and their tips ground against him like red-hot rubies. He released her hips.

She went into motion: side to side, up and down, round and round. Her need was to great and she was moving so rapidly that Fargo had no chance of matching her energy. He just had to let her go, and in only a minute or two she buried her face against his chest to keep from crying out as her body shuddered with wave after wave of pleasure.

After a while her breathing slowed, and she lay still against him and gathered her strength.

"I know that wasn't much good for you," she said at last.

"It was good," Fargo said. "I just didn't get to finish."

"I know, and I'm sorry. But you didn't have any letdown. I can still feel you inside me. It feels good, Fargo. If you can wait a minute, we'll do it again. For you, this time."

Fargo said he could wait, but it didn't take even a minute. He felt her nipples growing hard against him, and the sensation made him grow a bit as well.

"My God," Abby said. "I didn't know it could get any bigger. Oh, my."

She moved tentatively, drawing herself up so far that only the tip of his shaft remained inside her. She twirled slightly, then lowered herself very, very slowly, allowing Fargo to feel the sensation along the entire length of himself.

"Ah," she said. "Ah. That's good. That's good."

Fargo agreed, but didn't say so. He lay back and let her work, slowly at first and then faster and faster as she grew more and more excited. Soon she was practically bouncing on him, and he put his hands to the curve of her hips to keep her from flying off.

"Hurry, Fargo," she said. "Hurry, I'm going off again!"

This time Fargo wasn't going to let her finish without him. He slowed her down so that he could match her eager thrusting, moving with her until he could feel the pent-up flow ready to burst its dam.

"Now," he said, releasing her hips, and she gyrated like a snake on a griddle.

"Ah, yes, ah!" she said. "Oh, oh, oh!"

As she reached the height of her passion, Fargo exploded inside her, gushing hot bursts, one after the other like cannon fire. Her own climax shook her, and every time he shot, she moaned with satisfaction.

This time she made no attempt to smother her voice, but Fargo was too far gone to care. If the entire Murray gang had burst into the room at that moment, he wouldn't have been able to do a thing to save himself.

When they were both spent, Abby rolled off him and they lay almost enveloped in the soft mattress.

"I know you think I'm awful," she said after a few minutes. "I don't know what got into me."

"I did," Fargo said, and she hit him on the shoulder.

"That's not what I mean. I mean, I never thought I'd be doing . . . that . . . with a man I hardly know. I didn't do it with Jed until months after we met. And he's the only other one."

She started to cry softly, and Fargo said, "Jed would understand. It's nothing for you to worry yourself about."

"I hope you're right. But even if he wouldn't, I needed it. I just didn't know how much. Thank you, Fargo."

"I'm the one who should be doing the thanking."

Abby got out of the bed and slipped her nightgown back over her head.

"You don't owe me any thanks." She was back in control of herself now. She seemed almost like a different person, more remote than any time since Fargo had met her. "I won't be back for another visit. I hope you understand."

"I think I do," Fargo said. "But if you change your mind, don't forget where I am."

He thought he saw her smile, but in the darkness he couldn't quite be sure.

"I won't forget," she said.

Fargo was asleep and dreaming, swallowed up in the softness of the mattress.

He was a child again, almost a young man, and he was surrounded by death. He was the only one left, the only one who could avenge them, and he swore that he'd do it if it took him the rest of his life. It seemed so real, the screaming, the crashing of glass as—

The crashing of glass was real, and Fargo jerked awake to see the burning torch that lay on the floor by the bed. It had come in through the broken window, and the screaming in his dream became the whooping and hollering of the Murray gang.

He heard gunfire, but by that time he was snuffing out the torch with a quilt that hung on a frame near the wash-stand. When the fire was out, he pulled on his pants and buckled on his own pistol.

Someone was beating on his door. He opened it to see Abby standing there. She was holding a lamp and still wore her nightgown.

"It's the Murrays," she said.

Fargo had figured that out. He asked about Lem.

"He and the others are stumbling around in the kitchen. They won't be much help."

"Any damage?"

"Somebody threw a torch in the kitchen window. It didn't do any damage."

"They might be going for the barn. I'll see if there's anything I can do."

"Be careful," Abby said.

Fargo left her there and went out on the porch. Sure enough, the Murray gang had moved on to the barn. Fargo could see them moving around in the torchlight. Several of them were off their horses, piling something that looked like it might be hay around the building. Fargo figured they'd set the hay afire if they got the chance.

The barn was too far away for Fargo to hit anybody with a pistol shot unless he got lucky, but he thought he could distract them, maybe even chase them away. Not that he had much hope of that, but he fired the Colt three times.

Nobody fell, but three men turned and looked back toward the house. One of them dropped the torch he was holding and pulled a rifle from a saddle holster. The moon had gone down, and Fargo could have been nothing more than a dark blot to the man, but the Trailsman nevertheless thought it was time for him to find some cover.

There was nowhere to hide, however. When Fargo turned, he saw someone standing by the porch of the house. It wasn't anyone from inside. There was a muzzle flash, a crash of sound, and something kicked Fargo like the biggest mule in the world.

Then everything went black.

5

Fargo came to, sputtering. Someone was pouring water on his face, nearly drowning him. The Trailsman sat up coughing. When he'd cleared the water out of his mouth, he said, "That's enough dammit."

He wiped water from his eyes and looked up at Lem, who was holding a crockery jar.

"I thought at first you were dead," Lem said. "But then I could see you were breathing. You're just grazed."

Now that consciousness was returning, Fargo's head felt like it had been split open with an ax. He put his fingers to the left side of it, and they came away sticky with blood.

"Some son of a bitch shot you," Lem said. "Probably thought you were dead same as I did, or else he'd have finished the job. You're lucky he didn't."

Fargo didn't feel lucky. He managed to stand up, but he had to put out a hand and grab Lem's shoulder to steady himself.

"Where's Abby?" he asked.

"Gone," Lem said. "Those goddamned Murrays took her."

Fargo's head throbbed. He looked at the barn. It wasn't burning, and he realized that he'd been tricked. The gang had fired shots at the house and thrown in a couple of torches to get his attention. When he'd come out of the house, he'd been fooled by the men at the barn into thinking they were the ones who'd be trouble. But the trouble had been behind him. The Murrays didn't want to burn Lem's barn. Peter Murray hadn't lost a barn; he'd lost a son. So he'd taken Lem's daughter in return.

"Is she alive?" Fargo said.

34

"She's alive, for now. She might wish she wasn't. If I hadn't been half drunk, maybe I could have stopped them. Abby's not the only one missing."

"Ellis and Tabor?"

"Hell, those two are all right. Still trying to wake up. They weren't any more help to Abby than I was. No more help to Jed, either. That's who else is missing, Fargo. They came in and took Jed's body. What are we going to do about it?"

Fargo wasn't sure how he'd become the man with the answers, and his head hurt too much for him to think. He touched his wound again.

"You come on in the house, and we'll put something on that," Lem said, taking Fargo's elbow. "Then we'll figure out what to do."

Fargo let himself be led inside, but he was afraid they were wasting valuable time. If Abby was alive, there was no telling what Murray might do to her. There was no need to worry about Jed. They couldn't do anything to him that would matter to anyone now, least of all Jed.

Lem took the Trailsman into the kitchen. Jed's body was gone from the table. In the flickering lantern light, Fargo saw that an empty whiskey bottle lay on the floor not far away. Ellis and Tabor sat in their chairs and looked up woozily. Tabor rubbed his bald head and groaned as if his head might be throbbing as much as Fargo's.

"Don't mind those two," Lem said, rummanging around in the wood box. He raised up with another bottle of whiskey, about half full. He held it to the lantern light and shook it slightly, as if to appraise its contents. "Sure hate to waste good whiskey, but you need this more than we do. Come on over here."

Fargo walked over, and Lem uncorked the bottle with his teeth. With his free hand, he tilted Fargo's head at an angle and then poured whiskey on the wound. It stung like hell, and Fargo bit his lip. It was all he could do to stand still. Whiskey ran into his eyes, but he hardly felt it because of the other pain.

"Just hang on there for a minute," Lem said, and went out of the room.

On his way he handed the whiskey bottle to Tabor, who

took a quick drink. He shook his head like an angry dog and passed the bottle on to Ellis, who just held it and looked at it.

When Lem came back, he wrapped a piece of clean cloth around Fargo's head and tied it in back.

"That ought to take care of you," he said. "You're might damn lucky. And your head must be hard as an oak root."

"So I've been told before," Fargo said.

His head was pounding a little less now, and he became more aware of things. The first thing he realized was that he didn't have his Colt any longer.

"It's lying out there where you fell," Lem said when he saw Fargo reach to the empty holster. "I should have brought it in."

"I'll get it," Fargo said. "What about my horse?"

Fargo's big Ovaro stallion was in a little corral out behind the barn, along with Lem's mules, Jed's horse, and a couple of cows.

"Still where it was, as far as I know. Have you decided what we're going to do?"

Fargo hadn't answered that question the first time Lem asked it, and he wasn't sure he could this time, so he asked a question of his own instead.

"Which way did Murray go?"

"Off down toward the creek. Tore through my corn with those horses of his and probably ruined half of it. I don't care about the damned corn, though. We've got to do something for Abby."

Fargo didn't think the *we* included Tabor and Ellis, neither of whom looked capable of walking, much less facing the Murrays. They'd had considerably more to drink than Lem, and they still hadn't said a word. Tabor sat looking at the floor. Ellis held the whiskey bottle and looked like he wanted another drink, but couldn't bring himself to take it.

"I have an idea what Murray might be up to," Fargo said. "I'll go have a look. You and your friends had better stay here."

"You won't be a match for that gang if they catch you."

Fargo knew that, but he didn't think having Lem and the others along would be any advantage. In fact, he was pretty sure they would be a hindrance.

"I'll try not to get caught," he said.

He started out of the kitchen. Tabor and Ellis watched him wordlessly.

"I'll get your gun and hat," Lem said, and followed him outside.

Fargo had been right about what the Murray gang was up to. They were gathered in the marshy bottomland, and some of them had been digging. There was only one body they'd be looking for, and it looked like they'd already found it. There were two dark bundles tied across the backs of a couple of horses. One of them was probably Jed, and the other, the recently unearthed Paul Murray.

Fargo had tied the Ovaro a good distance away and was hiding in some scrawny cottonwoods. He wasn't worried about being seen. It was too dark, and the light from the gang's torches didn't reach his spot. There was no danger of anyone hearing him. A ghost was noisy compared to Fargo.

He could see Abby, her hands tied behind her, standing in front of Angel Murray. Angel's long hair fell below her floppy hat, and she was holding a pistol in one hand, aiming it at Abby's head.

A couple of men were leaning on shovels next to the hole where Paul Murray had been buried. There was a big man standing next to them. He said, "Now that's done, and we have my son back. Let's get this over with."

Two men went to one of the bundles and pulled it off the horse. They held it upright between them, and Angel prodded Abby in the back with the pistol.

"Get on over there," Angel said, her voice ragged.

Abby stumbled as she walked toward Jed's body, and a man caught her arm to hold her up. She shook him off and walked on her own.

When she got to Jed, Murray came over, holding a piece of rope that he'd taken from a saddle.

"Put your arms around your husband," he said.

Abby looked at him as if she couldn't believe what he had said.

"He's not my husband. And now he never will be, thanks to you."

"He's as close to a husband as you'll ever have," Angel told her. "Hug the son of a bitch. You and he are going to be real close for a long time, just like being married."

Fargo knew then what Murray had in mind, but he didn't know what he could do to prevent it. Murray had twelve men, thirteen if Angel counted. And Fargo had a feeling that in a fight she certainly would count. There wasn't much a man with a pistol could do against thirteen others even with the advantage of surprise.

Abby stood still, so Angel holstered her pistol and shoved her from behind, pushing her right up against Jed. Abby recoiled, but Angel kept both hands to her back, holding her in place. Abby struggled, but Angel was strong, and she pressed her up against Jed while Murray wrapped the rope around her and the corpse.

When he'd made three or four turns, he pulled it tight. Then he tied it in a knot and said, "Throw them in the hole."

"No!" Abby said. "You can't do that."

Murray chuckled. "I was beginning to think you were tough. But you aren't so tough after all." He paused and looked over at the open grave. "You killed my son. You buried him out here without even a marker. And now you're telling me what I can't do. Well, let me tell you something. I can do anything I damn well please." He looked around at his men. "Now, do what I said. Throw them in the hole."

The two men who had been holding Jed upright dragged his body, with Abby now tied to it, toward the grave. When they got to the edge, they paused, and Murray said, "God-dammit, throw them in."

Abby squirmed, but she didn't cry or scream. Fargo got the impression that Murray would have been happier if she had done one or the other. Or both. Her feet could get no purchase in the freshly turned earth as she tried to dig them in. She succeeded only in kicking a little dirt into the hole. The two men let go of Jed's arms and gave his body a gentle push. Abby tumbled backward into the grave, Jed on top of her.

Still Abby did not cry out. Fargo thought she had plenty of gumption. He wasn't sure he'd have been so quiet in her situation.

"Cover 'em up," Murray said.

The two men with shovels began tossing dirt into the grave. Murray and Angel walked over to watch.

"Serves the bitch right," Angel said. "Paul was worth more than the two of them put together."

"They're put together now," Murray said. "And that's the way they're going to stay."

He reached over and took a shovel from one of the men and handed it to Angel. Then he took the other one for himself. No one spoke as father and daughter shoveled dirt into the grave. The only sound was that of nightbirds in the trees and the earth as it hit the two bodies down in the hole.

When he and Angel finished, Murray gave the earth a couple of whacks. He tossed the shovel to the man who'd held it earlier and said, "That does it. Let's light a shuck."

Angel handed her shovel to another man and said, "How long do you think she'll last?"

"What the hell do I care?" Murray said. "I expect she's dead already."

"I hope not," Angel said. "I like to think she's still alive and thinking about how much longer she has before she stops breathing."

"Think whatever makes you happy," Murray said.

He swung into the saddle and rode away. His men followed. Angel lingered behind for a second or two, staring at the grave, and then turned her horse's head and rode after them.

6

As soon as the Murray gang was out of sight, Fargo came out of the trees at a run. He went to the grave and began digging with his hands, throwing dirt and talking loud in the hope that Abby could somehow hear him.

He knew that Abby had landed underneath Jed's body and that at least some air would have been trapped around her. The dirt was loose enough to trap a little more air, and the grave had not been dug deep the first time. Fargo was sure Murray's men hadn't deepened it, which meant that Abby was only a couple of feet under the soil. If Fargo was lucky—if Abby was lucky—he would reach her in time.

When he came to Jed, Fargo raked dirt aside even faster.

"Hang on a little longer, Abby," he said. "I'm nearly there."

He located Jed's back. Abby, being much shorter, would be right there.

"Don't talk," Fargo said, though he'd heard nothing from Abby. "Save your breath."

He cleared away more and more dirt, and soon he had Jed uncovered completely. Fargo straddled the grave, bent down, and grabbed Jed's belt. He braced his legs and pulled.

Jed and Abby came up out of the ground slowly, sinking back a little bit every time they rose, like a bad tooth being pulled from a jaw. Fargo's face reddened with strain, and his head began to throb steadily. After he had pulled them out a short distance, he could feel Abby helping him as she pushed with her legs.

"Glad to know you're alive," he said in response to her exertions. "I'll have you out in a second now."

He stumbled back, falling as they popped out of the earth. He heard Abby spluttering and spitting dirt. Reaching into his boot, he pulled out a bowie knife and cut the rope that bound her to Jed. Then he rolled Jed's body to the side.

Abby sat up, shaking dirt from her hair, brushing away from her face, still spitting. When she was finally able to talk, she said, "I thought I was going to die there."

"You didn't, though," Fargo said.

"How did you know where I was?"

"I saw them bury you."

Abby looked at him. Her cotton gown was filthy, her face was smeared with dirt, and her hair was matted with it.

"You saw them?"

"Yes. There wasn't anything I could do to stop them. There were too many of them."

"You bastard!" she said, leaning toward him, beating him with her tiny fists. "You let them bury me, you bastard!"

Fargo let her pound him. She was too small to hurt him unless she hit his wound, and there wasn't much chance of that.

After a while she was exhausted, and she collapsed against him.

"They told me you were dead," she said. "Angel told me that she'd killed you. She said that no one would come for me, that no one would ever find me."

"I found you," Fargo said. "I figured they'd come here, so I got here as soon as I could. I just didn't know what they'd do to you."

"I thought I was going to die. I thought I was going to lie there forever rotting away with Jed tied to me.

"It didn't happen," Fargo said.

She pulled away from him and looked at him more closely.

"What happened to your head?"

"That's where Angel shot me. But she didn't finish the job. She must have a soft heart."

Abby almost managed a smile. She said, "She might have a soft spot or two, but her heart's not one of them."

Fargo thought about the way Angel's breasts had felt when he'd encountered her in the barn earlier.

"I guess not," he said. "I'd better take you home now."

He stood up and helped her to her feet.

"They'll be back," she said. "The Murrays, I mean. They won't let it go at this, not when they find out that I'm still alive. You know that, don't you?"

Fargo said he knew. He told her to wait there while he went for his horse.

When he got back, she was standing by Jed's body.

"It wasn't enough for them to kill Jed," she said. "The way they talked when they brought me here, that didn't count for a thing. The only thing they cared about was that Paul Murray was dead."

Fargo bent down and took hold of Jed's body, grabbing it under the armpits from behind and pulling upright.

"They didn't care about Jed at all," Abby said, not looking directly at either Fargo or the body. "They thought his death didn't mean a thing."

"Families are important," Fargo said as he heaved Jed's body across the broad rear of the Ovaro behind the saddle.

"What about me and Jed?" Abby said. "If you care about your own family, you should care about other people's families."

Fargo knew that revenge didn't work that way, but he didn't try to explain things to her.

"It's a shame about the way they treated Jed," Abby said. "And Paul Murray, too. You ought to be allowed a little dignity when you're dead."

Fargo looked at Jed's body as it hung slack across the back of the horse. As far as Fargo had ever been able to tell, there wasn't a whole lot of dignity in death, and nothing Abby thought was going to change that. The way to look at it was that the things that had happened to Jed's body didn't matter to him in the least, any more than what had happened to Paul Murray's body mattered to Paul. When you were dead, if you felt anything at all, which Fargo doubted, you sure as hell wouldn't be worried about what was happening to a body you no longer had any use for. Or that was the way it had always seemed to Fargo.

But that wasn't anything he wanted to talk about with anybody, not then, so he put his foot in the stirrup, grabbed the saddle horn, and pulled himself atop the Ovaro. He reached down and offered his hand to Abby. She took hold of it, and he pulled her up in front of him.

"Let's get you back to the house," he said.

"Angel was the worst," Abby said as they rode through the ruined cornfield.

The green stalks were flattened and trampled in a broad path, though the damage wasn't as bad as Fargo would have expected.

"She was enjoying the whole thing," Abby went on. "She laughed the whole way to the graves, thinking about what they were going to do to me. She said that I took Jed away from her, and that he deserved what he got and that if she couldn't have him, nobody would. She said he and I were going to be together for a long time, but that it wouldn't be like I'd thought it would. I didn't know what she meant at the time."

"Did she tell you?"

"No. She said the men were all going to rape me, and she was going to watch. I think she would have liked that. It would have been another way to get back at me for marrying Jed. Thank God it was a lie, or maybe they just didn't have time for it. What they did was almost as bad. It would have been worse if you hadn't been there. I'm sorry I hit you."

"You didn't hurt me. Anyway, I don't much blame you. If somebody left me to be buried alive, I might get a little upset, myself."

Dawn was beginning to show in the eastern sky as a thin line of lighter gray. Somewhere off in the distance a dog was barking, faint and far away. Fargo knew there were other farms near the Watkins place, but he didn't know where they were.

"The Murrays aren't through with us, you know," Abby said. "They'll find out that they didn't kill you. They'll find out I'm alive. And when they do, they won't be happy about it. They might stew about it for a while, but then they'll come back."

"I wouldn't be surprised," Fargo said.

The funeral service was late that afternoon. It was a short one. Jed hadn't been much of a churchgoing man, so the preacher didn't have much to say.

They buried Jed in the churchyard in the stout wooden

43

casket that Cass Ellis had built that morning. Fargo could smell the newly sawed wood and the newly turned earth.

There were several markers in the cemetery, but Fargo didn't bother to count them or to read any of the inscriptions. They wouldn't have meant anything to him.

The little church was whitewash and clean, and the lowering sun pushed the building's shadow across the grass. People stood around the grave as the preacher read the Bible verse about the valley of the shadow of death. Fargo had heard it before.

He looked around at the men with their hats in their hands, the women crying under their bonnets. He recognized Alf Wesley, Rip Johnson, Frank Conner, and Tom Talley. Cass Ellis and Bob Tabor stood a bit farther off. They appeared to have recovered from their little drinking bout of the night before. Ellis had a couple of small cuts on his hands from having built the casket. He'd probably had a little case of the shakes.

Molly Doyle was there, too, dressed in clean men's clothing that did nothing to hide her abundant womanliness. She was crying quietly and trying to hide the fact by putting a hand to her face.

Abby and Lem were standing beside the preacher. There were tears on Abby's cheeks, but she wasn't weeping. She had cleaned herself up and washed her hair. There were no physical signs remaining of what had happened to her earlier, but Fargo wondered what might lie beneath the nearly placid surface of her face. A woman doesn't lose her prospective husband and then get thrown in a shallow grave tied to his body without it having some kind of effect.

The preacher finished reading the psalm, closed his Bible, and said a prayer. When he finished, several amens echoed his own. Some of the men who had dug the grave that morning got shovels from beside the church and began filling the grave.

Abby and Lem watched for a while and then turned away. The other mourners offered their condolences, while Fargo went over and sat on the church steps. After a few minutes, he was joined by Molly Doyle. She sat beside him without waiting for an invitation, the way another man might.

"What do you think will happen now?" she said.

"Why does everyone seem to think I know what's going to happen or how to deal with it?" Fargo asked.

Molly laughed. "I think you know the answer to that. You look like the kind of man who's been in a fracas or two before. The rest of these fellas around here, well, they look like farmers. Which is what they are. You give 'em a plow or some chicken feed, and they know exactly what to do with it. But you hand 'em a gun, and they're as likely to shoot themselves in the toe as to hit somebody who's shooting at them. I get the idea that wouldn't happen to you."

"I didn't sign on to be the sheriff. You have one of those?"

"We have us one, but you won't be seeing him. He'd never go up against the Murrays. You know about what's going on around here?

Fargo said he had a pretty good idea.

"Well, then you know what it's like. We have the army fighting the militia half the time and the militia fighting the army the other half. Most of the folks here don't want any part of that slavery argument, but that doesn't stop the fighting among the rest of them. The Murray gang just takes advantage of the situation to pretty much have a free hand. The army's too busy to mess with them, and the sheriff's too worried about his own skin."

"Sounds like you need a better sheriff."

"Nobody wants the job. The one we have's fine for rounding up drunks in town on Saturday night or tracking down somebody who's stolen a cow or some chickens. But that's all he's good for. Maybe you'd be interested."

Fargo said he didn't think so. He looked over at a spot near the church where Wesley, Conner, Talley, and Johnson were talking and smoking. Johnson smoked a pipe. The others had cigarettes.

"What can you tell me about those four?" Fargo asked.

Molly gave them a disdainful glance. It was plain that she didn't think much of them.

"What do you want to know about them? They're farmers, and that's about all you can say for them. Not very good farmers, either, but they get by."

The last was said with a bit of pride, but then Fargo already knew that Molly was proud of her own capabilities when it came to farming.

"You told me at the dance that Conner wasn't much and that he wanted to marry Abby to get Lem's place. What about the others?"

"Rip Johnson's married, got a place that could be right nice if he'd work it right. But he's as lazy as Conner. I feel sorry for his wife. She's just a little bit of a thing, but she does more of the work around there than he does."

"He has a hardworking wife, but you say he likes Abby."

"Everybody likes her. She's sweet and pretty and friendly. Why wouldn't they like her?"

"I didn't mean he liked her that way," Fargo said.

Molly frowned. "I know what you meant. Johnson's a sorry excuse for a husband. He thinks his wife doesn't know about him, but I'm sure she does. He'll make a grab for anything in skirts." She smiled and ran a hand over her well-filled shirt. "Or even some people who aren't in skirts."

Fargo grinned. "I take it he's made a grab or two for you, then."

"For all the good it did him. I told him if he tried anything like that again, I'd break both his arms, and I could do it, too."

Molly flexed her hands, and Fargo thought they were big enough to do just about anything she wanted to do with them. They weren't soft, womanly hands. They were roughened and callused from hard work.

"I know I'm not pretty," Molly said. "But that doesn't mean I'll let any man who comes along jump me. Rip found that out right quick. 'Course, I'm sure there's more than one who hasn't turned him down, married or not."

Molly didn't have a high enough opinion of herself, Fargo thought. She might not be small, like Abby, or have Abby's delicate features, but she was pretty enough in her own way. If she wouldn't hide her figure inside men's clothes, she'd most likely knock any man's eye out.

"And how about Wesley?" Fargo said.

"Alf? Well, he's not really so bad. He liked Abby, too, like the rest of them, but he was never a pest about it like Rip and Frank."

"What about Tom Talley?"

"He's a funny-looking fella, don't you think? Looks like somebody mashed his head in on the sides and crowded everything together."

"I don't much care how he looks. I'd like to know about him and Abby."

"What do you think?"

"If he's like everybody else, he must have liked her."

"Yes, but he knew he didn't have a chance with her. He tried to court her once, and she just laughed at him. Because of the way he looked, I guess. He pouted around for a couple of weeks after that, but he got over it."

Fargo wondered if that was true. Men didn't always get over things like that as easily as women seemed to think. Having a woman laugh at your looks was enough to set some men off, maybe even enough for them to start thinking about a way to strike back. It was possible that Talley had found a way, by killing Jed.

Women didn't get over things so easily, either. Fargo wondered if Molly had gotten over Jed, but he didn't ask. He said, "How did Jed take it that all these men were interested in his sweetheart?"

"He didn't like it one little bit, but there wasn't much he could say about it. After all, he was sweet on Angel Murray for a while there himself, at least until he found out what her family was involved in. So he couldn't really blame anybody for being interested in Abby. They knew her before he did, and I think they were all put out that she picked him over one of them. Made them all pretty mad when it happened. But they forgot about it after a while.

Again, Fargo wasn't so sure it was as easy as all that. But again he didn't press the point. He said, "Angel Murray didn't get over losing Jed quite so easy, by all accounts."

"Angel's no farmer, though. She's different. She's a killer. She's as bloodthirsty as her father. Maybe even worse than he is. And you know what they say about a woman scorned. In Angel's case, that's the literal truth. Compared to what she'd do to you, the devil in hell would probably seem like a nice Methodist preacher."

If that was true of Angel Murray, and Fargo didn't doubt

47

it, it was true in plenty of other cases, too. Fargo had known more than one woman who'd killed for a lesser offense than being scorned. He still wasn't convinced that any of the Murray gang had killed Jed, but if one of them had, it was probably Angel.

"Have you talked to Abby today?" he asked.

"You mean do I know about what happened to her last night? Yes, she told me. That's what I mean about Angel being bloodthirsty."

"And those farmers aren't bloodthirsty."

"Nope. Not a one of them. They just don't have it in them to be like that. You can call them a lot of things. Mean, some of them. Lazy, too, some of them. But not bloodthirsty."

"None of them ever got into an argument or a fight with Jed about Abby or about anything else?"

"Not that I know of. Like I say, they're not the fighting kind. You should ask Abby about it, though. She could tell you if there was ever any trouble."

"I'll do that," Fargo said.

He stared out over the cemetery. The grave had been filled, and the grave diggers were putting their shovels away in the undertaker's wagon. All that was left to remind anyone of Jed was a mound of fresh earth that would eventually sink back level with the rest of the ground and maybe a little below that. Grass would grow over it, and there would be another white marker to remind people that someone who'd once had a name was buried there.

The sun was going down behind a slate-gray cloud just above the horizon. The sky above the cloud was red and pink and yellow.

And on the horizon just off to the right, a thick column of dark smoke rose lazily upward.

Fargo pointed it out to Molly, who jumped to her feet.

"Son of a bitch!" she said. "That's my farm!"

7

Everybody who didn't have a horse piled into wagons and buckboards, and lit out for Molly's farm.

Molly was in the lead, riding a bay that was almost a match for Fargo's Ovaro. The Trailsman didn't try to overtake her, however. She deserved at least a few minutes alone when she reached whatever was going to be left of her farm. Fargo didn't think there would be much.

And he was right. When he got there, not long after Molly, the farmhouse was nothing but a chimney, a heap of smoking ashes, and a few smoldering boards that hadn't fallen over yet. Red spots glowed in the boards, and there was still some smoke wafting around. The air was thick with the smell of it.

Dead birds lay scattered all around the chicken yard, blown to pieces, blood all over the white feathers as if the birds had been used for target practice by Murray's men, which was probably close to the truth.

There had been a flower bed in front of the house, and the Murrays had ridden their horses through it destroying all the plants, leaving nothing standing, which was also pretty much true of the cornfield. They'd probably ridden through that while the house was burning, having themselves a high old time.

For some reason the barn, which was smaller than the one at Lem's, hadn't been burned. But there were two dead mules lying not far from it, both of them shot through one eye, their legs sticking out stiffly.

Molly was standing beside her horse when Fargo rode up. Her eyes were dry, and her face was drawn into hard lines.

"Those son of a bitch Murrays did this," she said.

"Why?" Fargo asked. "What did you do to them?"

"You don't have to do anything to them. They'd burn a house just for the meanness of it. But what I did was help bury Paul last night. They'll do something to everybody who had a hand in it, sooner or later."

Fargo thought over what she'd just said. There was something about it that bothered him.

"How will they know who helped?" he asked.

Molly turned slowly and looked up at him. Her eyes were hard and dark.

"You've asked a lot of questions today, Fargo, but that's the best one of all. How the hell *did* they know?"

She was going to say more, but by then some of the others on horseback were beginning to arrive, and Molly turned back to the rubble that had been her house. Maybe there were other reasons why the Murrays had it in for Molly. None of them had been there when Paul was buried. Someone could have been watching, but Fargo didn't think that was the case. He would have known.

Fargo caught a flicker of movement out of the corner of his eye and took a glance over toward the barn. The door was open, but Fargo didn't think the Murrays would have left anything alive inside.

"Get on your horse," Fargo told Molly. "Don't say anything. Just get out of here. Do it now."

She looked at him as if she didn't have any intention of leaving, but the urgency of his tone must have convinced her. She mounted up and did what he said as he went around telling the others who had arrived the same thing.

He wasn't sure he'd get away with it, and he didn't. Before he'd managed to get everyone started away, the first shot came from the barn.

Tom Talley was hit and fell off his horse. The gunshot helped people who had lingered figure out why Fargo was warning them, and they started riding away, yelling at those in the slower wagons and buggies to turn around.

By that time there were more shots coming from the barn, and seven or eight of the Murray gang came riding out from behind it, pistols firing.

Fargo had his Colt out, and he returned their fire. Farmers didn't generally take weapons to funerals, which of course the Murrays had counted on, and Fargo figured he was pretty much on his own. The odds weren't exactly fair.

The Murrays wouldn't care about that in the least, unless it was to be glad of it. They'd ride Fargo down and go right on after the others, killing as many as they could.

Or that's what they'd do unless Fargo could do something to stop them. Stopping them was a good idea, except he didn't have any idea how to stop that many men.

Of course one of them was a woman. Angel Murray was one of the riders charging at Fargo. She was beside her father, a wild grin of exhilaration on her face, and she was firing a pistol just like the rest. A bullet buzzed by Fargo's ear. Another one tugged at his shirt.

There was only one thing he could do. He wasn't sure it would work. In fact, he was almost certain it wouldn't. But he didn't have a lot of choice, so he did it.

He shot Angel Murray.

She fell from her horse and hit the ground hard. Fargo was running straight toward her before the other gang members even knew she was shot. They must have thought he was crazy, charging them like someone who believed he had them outnumbered instead of waiting for them to ride right over him.

They were so surprised that they couldn't shoot straight. Their bullets went far over his head, and he managed to shoot two more of them out of the saddle before he reached the spot where Angel was lying on the ground.

The others he'd shot were dead, but Angel was still alive, which was part of Fargo's admittedly shaky plan. There was a dark stain on the shoulder of her shirt where the bullet had struck her. Her hat had come off, and her black hair was spread out around her head.

Fargo reached down for her, grabbed hold of her good arm, and jerked her roughly to her feet. She screamed in pain, but Fargo didn't much care. In fact, he was glad she'd screamed. It let her father know that she was still alive.

As soon as she was upright, Fargo twisted her good arm behind her back. He stuck the barrel of his pistol right into the tender skin under her chin, pushing her head up so far that she was looking at the sky. The pistol barrel was hot. It burned her, and she yelled again, but not as loud as before.

The gang had given up on their pursuit of the farmers and turned back. The men in the barn came out, pistols at the ready.

Between the two groups, Fargo stood supporting Angel, with his pistol tight under her chin.

Peter Murray was getting close, so Fargo said, "That's far enough, Murray. Tell your men to keep their distance, or I pull the trigger."

Murray stopped, and although he gave no signal, so did all the others.

"You must be the one they call Fargo," Murray said, leaning forward casually in the saddle as if they were just two friends who'd met on the trail and were having a little talk.

Murray had a black beard shot through with white, and his hair, almost as long as his daughter's, hung below his hat. His eyes were as black as the ashes of Molly's house, but shinier.

"Well?" Murray said when Fargo didn't answer. "Is that your name or not?"

"It's my name," Fargo said. "Not that it matters. What matters is that if you want your daughter to stay alive, you need to get your men together and ride away from here. And not in the direction the farmers went."

"That's an interesting proposition. And what'll you do if I don't?"

"Your daughter's nothing to me," Fargo said. "I'll pull the trigger, and you'll get to see the top of her head come off."

Murray waved the pistol he was holding loosely in his right hand.

"What if I just shoot you instead?" he asked.

"You could do that," Fargo said. "But you'd still see the top of her head come off. You ought to know that. I have my finger on the trigger, and if you shoot me, there's no way in hell I won't pull it. Even if you kill me, I'll pull it."

Murray sat easy on his horse and looked over Fargo's head at the men who'd come from the barn. He nodded at them. They holstered their pistols and went to get their horses.

"Supposing I let you live," Murray said. "What then?"

"Your daughter lives, too."

"You mean you'll let her go, don't you? You live, I get my daughter back."

Fargo gave him a tight grin.

"No, Murray, that's not the way it works. I don't trust

you any more than I'd trust a diamondback rattler. As soon as I let her go, you'd gun me down where I stand. So you're not getting her back."

"If I'm not getting her back, then just what did you have in mind?"

"She goes with me. I see to it that her wound gets taken care of. When she's ready, she comes back to you."

Angel didn't seem to think much of the idea. She tried to pull herself out of Fargo's grasp, but he pushed her arm a little higher and kept the pistol barrel punched into her chin.

"She's got spirit, Fargo," Murray said. "But you're the one with the pistol."

"I guess that means you're going to take the deal."

"You don't trust me," Murray said. "But I'm supposed to trust you, is that what you're telling me?"

"That's about the size of it," Fargo said.

"Well, to hell with that, you son of a bitch. I'd lay odds you're the one killed my son last night, and today you've shot my daughter. And now you want me to trust you?"

"To tell you the truth, I don't give a damn whether you trust me or not. That doesn't have anything to do with it. We're talking about your daughter's life here, Murray. I shot her, but she's alive. That's more than I can say for the others I shot."

The two men lay not far from where Fargo stood. Neither of them had moved since hitting the ground, and they weren't likely to move ever again.

"If you don't let your daughter go with me," Fargo said, "she'll wind up as dead as they are. I don't see that you have much choice."

Angel spoke for the first time. "Kill the son of a bitch."

"You heard her Murray. Go ahead. Maybe it's worth a try. It's either that or ride away. Your choice."

Murray sat and thought it over. For all the anxiety that showed on his face, he might have been considering whether to wear a black shirt or a blue one.

"Suppose I go along with you," he said after a couple of long minutes had gone by. "How long do you keep her?"

"I told you. Until she's ready to ride away."

"That won't be long," Angel said. "You bastard."

Murray went on as if she hadn't spoken.

53

"And you'll just let her ride away?"

"You have my word on that."

"I don't know what your word's worth, Fargo, but it seems like I'm going to find out."

"Just make up your mind," Fargo said. "This pistol's getting heavy. My finger might slip."

"All right," Murray said. "I guess you have me over a barrel. But I have to warn you about something."

"What's that?" Fargo asked.

"If anything happens to Angel, I'm going to come after you and kill you. There won't be anything to stop me. And while I'm at it, I'll burn every house and barn and field within fifty miles. You have my word on that. And my word's good."

"I believe you," Fargo said, but Murray wasn't listening. He nodded at his men, and they rode past Fargo, joining the men who waited at the barn.

"You son of a bitch," Angel said. "Let go of my arm."

"Not yet," Fargo said. "I don't trust your father enough to do that."

"He's not going to do anything. Let go of me."

Murray and his men rode away without a backward glance. When Fargo judged they were out of firing range, he let go of Angel's arm, and she promptly fainted dead away. Which made it a lot easier for Fargo to throw her on a horse and take her away from there.

"You should've killed him," Molly said. "You had him right there, and you let him get away."

"If I'd killed him, there would still have been plenty of others to get rid of me and come after you," Fargo reminded her. "And come after everybody else, too."

"And you promised him you wouldn't kill Angel. Dammit, why did you have to do that?"

"Because I wanted to get out of there alive, for one thing, and I didn't want Murray killing everybody else, which is what he would have done."

"Damn. But you're probably right. I'll bet you always keep your promises, too, don't you."

Fargo nodded.

"I knew it. That's the kind of man you are. So you can't kill her. How about if I kill her?"

Fargo had to laugh at that. They were sitting in Lem's kitchen. Angel was in the bedroom where Fargo had spent the previous night. Lem and Abby were with her and the doctor who'd come from town. He didn't strike Fargo as much of a doctor, to tell the truth. His hands were shaky and his eyes were bloodshot. Lem had gone to town for him and had most likely found him in a saloon, if not lying drunk in an alley somewhere. But he was good enough to dig a bullet out of Angel's shoulder. It hurt her when he did, and Fargo heard her cry out once. But he didn't care.

"You can't kill her, either," Fargo said. "I don't think Murray would take kindly to that. He might think it's not part of our agreement."

"The son of a bitch burned my house. He killed my chickens and mules. He destroyed my corn crop."

Fargo understood how Molly felt. She still hadn't cried, as far as he knew, but she must have felt like it. She'd lost everything.

"He killed Tom Talley, too," Molly said.

Fargo didn't think that was the case, but he couldn't be sure who'd shot Talley. And it didn't matter, anyway. Talley was dead, and Murray was to blame whether he'd pulled the trigger or not.

"He ought to be punished for all that," Molly went on. "He can't just keep on raiding and killing and doing whatever he pleases."

"What about the army?" Fargo asked.

"The army's too busy, and the sheriff doesn't care. I told you that. I care, though."

Fargo cared, too. He didn't like the idea of Murray being able to run roughshod over an entire community. It wasn't Fargo's job to do anything about it, but because of Murray, Jed was dead, and Jed had been Fargo's friend. Fargo had lost friends before. None of them had gone without justice, however. Fargo wasn't one to let somebody kill a friend of his and get away with it.

"Maybe we can do something about that gang," Fargo told Molly. "But we'll have to do it later, and we can't do anything to Angel because I promised not to. When she's well and gone, though, we might be able to get Murray."

"How?" Molly asked.

Fargo wished he had an answer for that. But he didn't.

8

Fargo had to sleep in the barn that night. Angel was using the bed he'd had in the house, and Molly was staying in the kitchen.

"I've slept on harder beds than that table before," she'd said, and nobody mentioned that Jed had been laid out there only the previous evening. Fargo didn't think it would have bothered Molly even if anyone had brought it up.

The barn smelled of hay and manure, and no one would ever have guessed that a dance had been held there so recently. Fargo didn't mind the smell. He made himself a bed in the loft, laying his blanket over a pile of straw that he gathered up. He'd slept in worse places before.

After he got settled in, he lay back and thought about all that had happened since last night's dance. There were a lot of little things that bothered him about all of it, but he hadn't quite sorted it all out as yet. He was sure, however, that there was more going on with Murray and his gang than met the eye. Maybe he could have a little talk with Angel about it. Fargo chuckled at the thought. He might as well have a little talk with one of Molly's dead mules, for all Angel would tell him.

He drifted off to sleep, but, asleep or not, he was always on the alert. When the barn door creaked open, he came awake instantly.

His hand went to his pistol, which was right beside him in its holster. He pulled it out and waited. For a few seconds he heard nothing more, but then something scuffed a ladder rung below him. He thumbed back the hammer of the pistol.

It was dark inside the barn. Only the faintest moonlight filtered in through the cracks in the boards, but Fargo's eyes were used to the dark by that time, and in a few seconds he saw the dark outline of a head rise above the floor of the loft.

He let the hammer down quietly and said, "Is that you, Molly?"

"Yes." She climbed the rest of the way up the ladder and stepped into the loft. "How did you know?"

"I didn't until just now." Fargo slipped the pistol back into its holster. "You almost got yourself shot."

"That would have been too bad. But I didn't want to make too much noise getting here. I didn't want anybody to know I came. There's something we need to talk about."

Fargo sat up and said, "What's that?"

Molly walked the few paces to where he was and sat on the hay beside him.

"Talley's funeral," she said when she was settled.

"What about it?" Fargo asked.

"You know what happened when we buried Jed. Don't you think Murray might try the same thing again?"

Fargo hadn't thought about that, but now that she'd brought it up, it didn't seem very likely to him.

"He knows we're onto that trick," Fargo said. "He'd expect us to have somebody waiting at Talley's house. Besides, he might not even know Talley's dead."

"He knows. He knows everything that goes on around here. He probably even knew about the little stash of money I had in my house."

"You didn't mention any money."

"What good would it do to mention it? It's either burned up or Murray's got his dirty hands on it. It's gone, either way."

"If Murray took it, how did he know you had it?"

"The same way he knows everything else. Anyway, he might have burned the house, but you can bet he took everything that was worth taking before he set a torch to it."

"Does Talley have anything that's worth taking?"

"I don't know. But Murray probably does."

Fargo thought about that for a minute and said, "Talley wasn't married, was he?"

"No. Not too many women would have anything to do with him because of the way he looked. People put a lot of stock in looks, in case you haven't noticed. But then you wouldn't."

"Why wouldn't I?"

"Because big, good-looking galoots like you never think about things like that. You probably have women flocking around you like flies to a honey pot."

"It's not quite that bad," Fargo said, feeling a little uncomfortable. "But let's get back to Talley. If he wasn't married, who's looking out for his house tonight?"

"Nobody, probably. He didn't have any kin around here. They're all back east somewhere. He's laid out at Rip Johnson's place, and Rip and some of the others are sitting up with the body."

The two men that Fargo had killed didn't have anybody sitting up with them. Alf Wesley and some of the others had buried them with the others who'd been killed at the dance. At the rate Murray was losing men, he was going to have to find himself some new help before long, which wouldn't make him feel any kindlier toward Fargo.

"If there's nobody at Talley's place," Fargo said, "why would Murray wait until the funeral to go there?"

Molly sat up straighter beside him.

"I hadn't thought about that," she said. "Hell, Murray's probably over there right now. Maybe we could catch him." She stood up. "Come on, Fargo, let's go. We can't just let him take everything Talley had and then burn his place like he burned mine."

Fargo wasn't sure Murray would do anything of the kind.

"We have Angel," he reminded Molly. "Murray might not want to take the risk of doing something that would make us decide to go back on our bargain."

"What risk? If there's nobody there, who's to say Murray's to blame for anything that happens? Without any proof of what he'd done, you'd never go back on your word. Get up, Fargo. We can't let Murray get away with it."

Fargo stood up and brushed a little straw off his clothes. He didn't think Murray was going to get away with anything, and if he was, there was always the chance that he'd already done it. But Molly was insistent, and Fargo didn't have anything against a little midnight ride now that he was fully awake anyway.

"All right," he said. "Let's go see if there's any trouble going on."

"This time, I'll have a gun with me," Molly said, and

started down the ladder. She poked her head above the level of the loft and added, "Or two guns."

The night air was cool and dry. A light breeze was blowing, and now and then a thin cloud would scud across the face of the moon. But there was plenty of light for the horses to see by. Molly was on the bay, riding just ahead of Fargo and leading the way.

They passed a couple of farmhouses, and one of them had lights in several of the windows. Molly said that was Rip Johnson's place.

"He and Tom were never very good friends," she said. "Men didn't like Tom any better than women did. It was kind of Rip to sit up with him. Rip may be a son of a bitch, but he has his good points, few as they are."

They rode on for another half a mile before they came to a solitary house silvered by the moonlight and sitting near a cornfield. It seemed to Fargo that everybody in Kansas must be growing corn.

I hope Rip came over here and milked Tom's cow," Molly said as they neared the house.

"I don't hear any cows complaining," Fargo said. "So somebody must have milked her. And we'd better be quiet ourselves. We don't want Murray to hear us if he's around here."

Fargo didn't think there was any danger of that. If Murray had been there, there would have been some sign of him, but there was none. No horses near the house or barn, no lights showing in the windows. And no one had burned the house. There was always a chance someone had killed the milk cow, but Fargo didn't think that had happened.

"I guess I was wrong," Molly said. "But that doesn't mean Murray won't be coming along later. Or that he hasn't been here and cleaned out the house already. We'd better check inside and see if everything's all right."

They left their horses in the barn and walked to the house. When they went inside, Molly lit a lamp she found on a table near the door and they went through each of the small rooms. As far as Fargo could see, nothing looked disturbed or out of place. If Murray was going to do anything, he hadn't done it yet.

"I guess we were chasing the wrong rabbit," Molly said, setting the lamp down on the kitchen table. "But one of us ought to stay here for the rest of the night, just in case Murray does show up."

"I can stay," Fargo said.

"You mean you don't think it would be right for a woman to stay. Well, let me tell you something, Fargo, I'm as good a man as you are." Molly slapped at the Colt she was wearing, and the pistol seemed to jump into her hand. "See what I mean?"

"You're fast, all right," Fargo said. "But being fast doesn't mean a thing if you can't shoot."

"I can shoot. You want me to shoot something and prove it?"

"I'll take your word for it. But shooting at a target's not the same as shooting at somebody who's shooting back at you."

"You could always draw on me and find out if I could shoot back."

There was a seriousness in her voice that made Fargo wonder about her.

"You don't have to prove anything to me," he said.

"Then you're not like most men. They never want to believe I'm as good as they are."

"Maybe that scares them," Fargo said.

Molly spun the pistol once and put it back in the holster.

"Like I told you before," she said. "Most men are scared of a big woman. At least all these farmers around here are. They want their women to be little and dainty, which anyone can plainly see I'm not.

"And I said they might not know what they're missing."

"Yes, you did." Molly looked around the kitchen. "Are you interested in finding out? There's nobody here but us."

In most circumstances, Fargo wouldn't have hesitated to accept the offer. But these weren't most circumstances.

"What if Murray happens to show up?" he asked.

"Are you afraid of me, or of Murray? I didn't take you for a coward, Fargo."

Fargo was too old to get into that kind of argument. He said, "Do you think Talley would mind if we borrowed his bedroom? Or would you rather we went out to the barn?"

"I'd bet you a gold dollar that Talley hasn't ever used that bedroom for anything but sleeping in the eight or nine years he's lived here. We might as well break it in for him. He wouldn't mind, even if he was alive."

She picked up the lamp and walked out of the kitchen. After a couple of seconds had gone by, Fargo followed her.

She went into the bedroom and set the lamp on a washstand that held a pitcher and bowl. She raised the chimney and started to blow out the flame.

"Don't," Fargo said. "I want to have a look at you."

Molly's face reddened. "You right sure about that? There's a whole lot of me."

"That's what I want to look at."

Molly, looking a little uncertain, removed her gunbelt and set it beside the lamp. Then she started to undress.

The more she took off, the better she looked. The mannish clothing had managed to conceal the true bounty of her figure even from Fargo, who had a keen eye for that sort of thing. Her breasts were mountainous, but they stood proudly out from her chest without support, the nipples the size and color of ripe cherries. Her hips, though wide, were perfectly shaped. And the tangled triangle of hair at the juncture of her thighs was as inviting as any such bramble Fargo had ever seen.

"Well?" Molly said, pulling her hands on her hips and striking a pose. "Had yourself a good look?"

Fargo nodded. "Even better than I expected."

"Then you'd better show me how much you like it."

Fargo hurriedly took off his own clothing. His rod stood out stiff as a fireplace poker.

"Seems you must like it quite a bit," Molly said with a grin. "Judging by the size of that thing, you ought to be man enough to handle me; but if you are, you'll be one of the few."

"I guess we'll find out about that," Fargo said, walking over to her and letting the hot tip of his penis touch her stomach.

Molly reached for it and encircled it with her hand. She pulled him to her, pressing his hardness against her.

"That's as hot as a pistol barrel after a good fight," she said.

Fargo put his arms around her and pulled her closer, letting her feel the entire hot, hard length of him. Her breasts were soft as cotton, but they engorged and grew firmer as he held her. As they did, the tips stiffened and enlarged.

"Mmmmmm," Molly said, and Fargo kissed her.

61

He didn't have to bend to do it. She was nearly as tall as he was, and she joined the kiss with enthusiasm. Their tongues dueled for a moment, and Fargo found himself being dragged to the bed. Molly fell back on it, pulling him down on top of her. It wasn't a hard fall, cushioned as it was by her prodigious breasts.

She hugged him to her and kissed him again. Fargo let his hand wander to the mound between her legs, and his fingers entangled themselves in the crisply curling hairs. She pushed her ample hips back at the gentle pressure of his hand, and he let his finger slip into the soft cleft, already slick from her juices. He ran the tip of his finger over her moistened mound, and Molly's whole body spasmed with pleasure, so much so that his finger slipped inside her without any effort of his own part. As soon as it was inside, Molly clamped on it, and she rocked her hips wildly. She broke the kiss and started to whoop.

"YeeeeeHaaaaaaw! YeeeeeHaaaaaaw!"

Fargo hadn't thought she'd be a screamer. He hoped there was no one any closer than Rip Johnson's house, or their sleep was going to be seriously disturbed. If Molly got any louder, she might even wake up Tom Talley.

After a couple of seconds, Molly lay still. She said, "Damn, Fargo. You could teach these farmers around here a thing or two, I'll tell you that."

"I hope that wasn't all you wanted from me," Fargo said with a grin.

"You're damn right it wasn't. We're just getting started. Now, why don't you sit up."

Fargo wasn't quite sure what she wanted him to do, but with a little help and coaxing, he figured it out. He sat a-straddle of her on her stomach, and she held her breasts invitingly, her hands cupped on the sides.

"Stick it between them," she said. "I'd like to feel it rubbing them."

Fargo did as she asked, letting his throbbing shaft slide in between the soft mounds, so lightly slicked with sweat. Molly pressed them around him and said, "Pump it."

Fargo slid his penis into the crevice as far as he could and then withdrew it.

Molly gasped. "Faster," she said, and fondled her nipples, which seemed to grow even larger. "Faster."

Fargo obliged her. Her head tossed and her eyes closed. Fargo reached behind him and found the tangled triangle again. His finger slid easily down the wet track and into the hot honey hole that waited there.

Molly's mouth came open as she rocked under him.

"YeeeeHaaaaaaw! YeeHaw! YeeHaw! YeeHaw!"

She was flouncing so much that she nearly threw Fargo off and onto the floor. He was worried that Talley's bed wouldn't be able to take the punishment, but it help up until Molly was still again.

"You're even better than you look," Molly said finally. "But you're not getting as much out of this as I am."

"You might be surprised," Fargo said.

"I don't think so, but here's a surprise for you."

Fargo's lance was still pushed up between her breasts, and Molly leaned her head forward to take the tip of it in her mouth. She nursed and tongued it vigorously while rubbing her hands over her distended nipples. Fargo leaned back a bit and worked his finger between her legs.

She stopped her work and said breathlessly, "If you don't quit that, I'm not going to be able to finish you."

"I have an idea," Fargo said. "Let's both finish."

"That sounds mighty fine. Give it to me. Hurry."

Fargo slid down her ample frame until he was positioned between her legs. She was spread out invitingly, knees bent, hips already moving in anticipation, and he bent forward to take a nipple in his mouth. Each time he sucked it, she quivered.

"That feels wonderful," she said, "but you'd better—ahhhh!—get inside me. I can't wait much—ahhh!—longer."

Fargo didn't keep her waiting. He shoved inside all the way in one smooth stroke and lodged himself there. He felt her inner walls rippling around him, closing on him as they had on his finger. He waited for a moment, then started a slow slide out.

After a few leisurely strokes, he sped up, and Molly threw her legs around him, locking her ankles, urging him to go faster, faster.

Soon they were rocking together in such a frenzy that the bed began to bang against the wall, and Fargo thought it might break right on through.

There wasn't a thing he could do to stop it, however. He

felt a tremendous pressure building in him. It seemed to start in his toes and work its way all the way up his legs, which tightened like a bowstring."

"Please!" Molly said. "Please give it to me. Now! Now!"

Fargo gave it to her. In one last lunge he thrust into her as far as he could go as Molly screamed with joy.

"YeeeeeeeeeeeeeeeHaaaaaaaaaaaaaaaaaaaw!"

There were a few more screams, and when she finally subsided, they lay on the bed until their breathing returned to normal.

"My God, Fargo," Molly said. "I never knew anything could be like that. I don't guess there's any chance of you settling down and being a farmer, is there."

"That's not my line," Fargo said.

"I knew that. Too bad. You're going to miss out on a lot. And so am I."

"I told you these fellas around here didn't know what they were missing."

"I knew you were right. I just didn't know how right."

"Maybe if you gave one of them a chance, he'd do you some good."

"I doubt that any of them cares about a chance, except maybe for Rip Johnson, and he's as bad as a goat. He'd try for anybody or anything, but I don't mess with married men. Besides, on his best day he couldn't give me as good as what I just had. But maybe I ought not to be so choosy. A woman can get mighty lonesome living all by herself. I'd been wanting to do that a long time. None of the boneheads around here seemed likely to make an offer, though. They were too busy wishing that tiny little Abby Watkins would give them a tumble, which she never did for a one of them, not until Jed came along. And now that she's available again, nobody's going to give me a second look."

"Then they're crazy," Fargo said.

"I thank you for that. And for what we just did."

"The pleasure was mine," Fargo said. "Maybe not all of it, but plenty."

"I'm glad Murray wasn't here, and we could use the bed. Otherwise I might've had to get you back to Lem's and drag you down in that hayloft. Hay can be mighty itchy."

Fargo said that was the truth, and then they heard the first gunshots.

9

"Goddammit," Molly said as she tumbled off the bed. "Get dressed Fargo."

Fargo was already pulling on his shirt. He said, "How far away do you think those shots were?"

"Sound carries a long way out here, but I'd say at Rip's. They're after him instead of after Tom's stuff. We should've guessed."

"Why?" Fargo asked, pulling on his boots.

"Because everybody there at Rip's will be half drunk by now. All the men drink too much when they're sitting up with somebody, maybe because they're celebrating that it isn't them on the table. Murray knows all about that. I knew he wouldn't let us kill two of his men and do nothing about it. We have to get over there before it's too late."

They got their horses out of the barn and started off for Johnson's farm at a gallop. When they got there, Fargo didn't see any sign of Murray.

It was quiet for a few seconds, and Molly said, "What's going on? Is it over?"

"Just a lull," Fargo told her, and almost as soon as he said it, more shots were fired.

Fargo saw flashes from Johnson's cornfield as the Murray gang fired on the house. Now and then there would be an answering shot from the house, but it didn't seem to Fargo that there was a lot of resistance being put up.

The lamps were still on inside, and Fargo said, "They should have doused those lights. Every time somebody gets close to one, he's going to get shot."

"At least Murray hasn't burned the place down yet."

That surprised Fargo a little, considering that there'd

been plenty of time, and Johnson wasn't doing much fighting back.

"What are we going to do, Fargo?" Molly asked.

That question seemed to be asked a lot lately. Fargo said, "We can get behind Murray, but we'll have to be careful not to hit anybody in the house when the shooting starts."

"You don't have to worry about me," Molly said, pulling a shotgun from a leather case tied to her saddle. "This thing won't shoot that far, but it'll tear apart anybody who gets close enough."

"You don't want to get too close to that Murray bunch."

"I'm not worried about them. Once they see this gun, they'll keep their distance."

"We'll leave the horses here," Fargo said, sliding off the Ovaro.

He went quietly along the edge of the cornfield, with Molly right behind him. When he judged that they were far enough behind Murray and his men, he entered the tall green stalks and started down a row, trying not to make any noise. The breeze was already rustling the corn, and Fargo didn't think there was too much danger that he'd be heard. He was accustomed to moving silently in cover, but he didn't know about Molly.

He looked back to see her only a few steps behind him. She had been so quiet that he hadn't heard her himself, which was quite a compliment to her stalking skill. He turned back and followed the row until he figured they were right behind Murray's gang. He motioned Molly to him and whispered in her ear.

"When I give the signal, you cut loose with that shotgun. Let's hope they run the other way."

Fargo drew his Colt. He couldn't see anyone, but he heard movement ten or twelve rows in front of him. And then someone started shooting toward the house again.

Fargo nodded to Molly and started firing his Colt. He didn't like firing blind, but he was shooting low to avoid the house. It didn't matter whether he hit any of Murray's men or not, as long as they got to moving.

And they did. When the gang realized that they were caught in a crossfire, the men all started running for their horses, bolting through and over the corn, crushing some of the stalks to the ground and trampling them. Molly pulled her pistol and shot at the retreating figures, but Fargo headed for the house. It was pretty much a waste of bullets to shoot at someone running away from you, especially when something, even something flimsy like stalks of corn, was in the way.

Arriving at the house, Fargo saw a body on the porch. It wasn't Johnson. It was a woman. Johnson's wife, probably. Fargo didn't remember having met her at the dance or the funeral, but he couldn't think of anyone else it was likely to be.

"This is Skye Fargo," he called out. "And Molly Doyle is with me. I'm coming inside."

Molly walked up beside him and said, "I'm coming in, too. We've chased those damn Murrays for you, Rip."

It was only then that she saw the body on the porch.

"Damn. It's Sarah Johnson. And look there." Molly pointed to the rifle that Sarah had dropped when she fell. "She always did have more guts than Rip, by a long sight. But you'd think the son of a bitch would have kept her in the house."

"I know I'm to blame," Rip Johnson said, coming to stand in the doorway. "God knows, I do. I told her not to run out and shoot at them, but she wouldn't listen to me."

His words were slurred, and he slouched against the door frame as if he couldn't stand up without a little help. Another man's head was visible just over his shoulder. The man looked to Fargo to be in even worse shape than Rip.

"You're drunk," Molly told Rip. "You're too drunk to fight, and you had to let your wife do it for you. I ought to shoot you down like the sorry dog you are, Rip Johnson."

"Go ahead," Rip said, tears springing to his eyes. "I know I deserve it. I'm no good without Sarah. You might as well shoot me and bury me with her."

"Shooting's too good for you," Molly told him. "And don't feel so damn sorry for yourself. It's not manly. Who else is in there with you?"

Tears ran down Johnson's cheeks. "I . . . I'm not sure."

"It's me," said the man behind him. "I'm here."

"Is that you, Rufe Tolliver?"

"That's right, Molly. I don't feel so good. I think my head's gonna fall off."

"You drink enough of that skull-bustin' whiskey, and it

will," Molly said. "You'll look mighty damn funny without it, too. Anybody else in there?"

"Frank and Alf are in the kitchen. I think they're dead."

"We'd better see about them, Fargo. You go ahead and do it. I'll see what I can do for Sarah."

There wasn't anything she could do, and Fargo knew it, but he went on inside, pushing past the still weeping Johnson and the confused Tolliver, who shied away from him as if he thought Fargo might be going to hit him. Fargo would have if he'd thought it would do the man any good, but it wouldn't.

In the kitchen Tom Talley lay covered on the table, just as Jed had been. There were going to be a hell of a lot of funerals before all the fighting was over, Fargo thought, at least if what had happened so far was any indication.

Alf Wesley and Frank Conner also lay in the kitchen, but they were on the floor rather than the table. Fargo looked them over. There wasn't a mark on either of them. They were dead, true, but only dead drunk. He toed Conner with his boot. Conner stirred, turned over, and started to snore. Fargo went back outside.

Johnson and Tolliver sat on the porch. Johnson had his head in his hands. Tolliver stared vacantly out across the cornfield. Molly and Sarah were gone.

"Where's Molly?" Fargo asked.

"She took Sarah in," Johnson said without removing his head from his hands. "She wouldn't let me touch her."

Fargo didn't blame her. He said, "You got too drunk, Johnson. You let everybody else get even drunker. You should have thought about what might happen. And you shouldn't have let a woman do your fighting for you."

"We fought," Tolliver said. "We did as best we could."

Fargo went over, pulled Tolliver's pistol from the holster, and gave it a look.

"You fired two cartridges. That's not much of a fight. What about you, Johnson?"

Johnson raised his head and rubbed the back of his hand across his face, leaving a light streak of dirt.

It's none of your damn business what I did, Fargo. You just keep your hands away from my pistol."

"I don't have to look at it to know there weren't many shots fired from this house. It's a wonder Murray didn't kill

68

all of you and burn it to the ground. He would have, too, if Molly and I hadn't come when we did. You're a lucky man, Johnson."

"How can you say that when my wife's dead? You don't know a thing about it."

"Go have another drink," Fargo said. "Maybe it'll make you feel better." He left the two men sitting there and went to look for Molly.

She was in the bedroom. She had laid Sarah's body on the bed and pulled the spread up over it.

"Now they have someone else to sit up with," she said. "I feel sorry for Sarah, but I don't feel a damn thing for that woman-chasing Rip. Except that it should be him lying under that spread instead of Sarah."

Fargo didn't disagree with her.

"She must have run out there thinking she could scare them off," Molly said. "Didn't show much sense, did she?"

Fargo didn't disagree with that, either.

"She was a brave woman," Molly continued, "and I guess she thought she was defending her home, but sometimes you have to think it's better to stay alive than to be brave."

Fargo nodded.

"What in the hell is the matter with you?" Molly asked. "You forgotten how to talk?"

"I'm thinking," Fargo said, which was the truth.

"What is there to think about?"

"What if Murray decides to come back? We seemed to have scared him away mighty easy, don't you think?"

"I hadn't thought about it. We'd better get some of those sorry excuses for men sobered up so they can use their guns if Murray doubles back."

"We can try to get them sober," Fargo said. "Or you could go round up some decent help."

"That might be a better idea. You think you can handle things around here?"

Fargo grinned. "If Murray doesn't come back, all I have to deal with is two dead people and four drunks. I ought to be able to handle them."

"I guess you could at that. I'll go get Lem and some of the others." Molly started out of the bedroom, then turned back. "What am I going to tell Lem when he asks what you and I were doing over here?"

"Tell him the truth. That we went to Talley's to check on things, heard gunshots, and came over here."

"That's not the whole truth," Molly said.

Fargo thought about Abby. He didn't have any designs on her the way the rest of the male population did, but he didn't much want her to know about his little escapade with Molly. There were some things better not talked about to anybody.

"It's enough of the truth to tell him," he said. "I wouldn't want to drag your good name in the dirt."

"Maybe that's what I need," Molly said. "Might make my life a lot more exciting."

"I wouldn't count on that."

"Yeah. You're right. I'll just tell Lem the truth. Most of it, anyhow."

"I think that would be best," Fargo said.

In an hour or so, Molly was back. Lem was with her, along with some men that Fargo didn't know. It was almost daylight by then, and Fargo didn't think Murray would be back, but there was no use in taking any chances.

Behind the men on horseback there was a wagon. Two women were in it. They'd come to help Molly with Sarah.

"I wouldn't be having any big funeral for her," Fargo said. "Somebody needs to stay here in case Murray comes back, and somebody should be at Talley's place."

"I've sent a couple of men over there," Lem said. "They aren't much for fighting, but they can at least use a gun if they have to. I'll talk to Rip about having a small funeral. He'll see the sense of it."

"What about your place?" Fargo asked. "Who's taking care of things there?"

"Abby's there. She has a gun, and she knows how to use it. You don't have to worry about my place."

Fargo wasn't so sure. "Do you think we can trust Murray?"

"Doesn't matter if we can or can't. I said Abby had a gun. She's sitting in a chair in the room with Angel, and she's holding the gun pointed right at her. Even Murray's not crazy enough to mess in a situation like that."

"I hope you're right," Fargo said, wondering if Abby would pull the trigger.

"Abby's not afraid to shoot, if that's what's worrying you," Lem said. "You don't have to worry about that. Abby blames Angel for Jed being dead. If anybody comes close to the house, Angel's going to heaven."

"I don't think that's very likely," Fargo said.

Lem gave him a grin. "I just thought it sounded better than the truth. If there was ever a woman bound for hell, Angel's the one."

"Maybe I'd better ride over that way, just to be sure everything's all right. You can deal with Rip and his friends. I think Conner's still asleep, but Wesley's awake now."

"We'll have 'em in fighting shape in no time," Lem said.

"How much would you like to bet on that?"

"Not a damn thing."

Fargo nodded in agreement.

"Wouldn't be smart," he said.

Fargo found Abby sitting in the bedroom, just as Lem had said. But there were three big differences between what Lem had told him and what Fargo saw.

The first difference was that Abby wasn't pointing the pistol at Angel. Instead, Abby was asleep in the chair.

The second thing was that Abby didn't have a pistol in her hand at all. There was no pistol anywhere in the room, as far as Fargo could tell.

And the third difference, probably the biggest one of all, was that Angel Murray was gone.

10

"It's no wonder I went to sleep," Abby said when Fargo got her to wake up. "I didn't get much sleep at all."

She said it somewhat accusingly, and Fargo was willing to share the blame for her failure to stay awake even though he wasn't the one who'd paid a visit to her bedroom. And he didn't think it would be a good idea to remind her that he hadn't had much sleep that night, either. For that matter, he knew damn good and well that he wasn't going to tell her he'd had hardly any sleep at all since then. Come to think of it, he could have used a couple of hours on his blanket up in the hayloft, but he knew he wasn't going to get them.

"I don't blame you for what happened," Fargo said. "How long have you been asleep?"

"It couldn't have been long. And Angel must have waited until I was sleeping hard, because she couldn't have taken the gun out of my hand otherwise. Why?"

"Because we have to find her. If she gets back to Murray, he'll probably kill every farmer around here."

"Oh," Abby said. "And it will be my fault."

"It's not your fault. Anyway, she's hurt. She shouldn't be able to get very far. She'll be too weak from that gunshot wound. You stay here. I'll go after her."

Abby's mouth was set in a hard line. She opened it to say, "Not without me, you won't."

Fargo could tell she was determined, and he didn't try to stop her from following him. He went out to the barn to see if Abby's horse was missing, but it was there. Angel probably hadn't been able to lift the saddle with her wounded shoulder. He looked around the barn to see if

72

Angel had hidden somewhere in a stall or the loft, but there was no indication that she'd even been there. Fargo went back outside, with Abby at his heels.

The sun was coming up, reddening the eastern sky over a low cloud bank and giving Fargo just enough light to see the ground, which was too hard to take any tracks. He did, however, notice some light dew that had been disturbed where someone had walked toward the cornfield. It was the only place of concealment around other than the barn.

"I'm going in there to look for her," Fargo said. "You wait here."

"No," Abby said. "I feel responsible. I'm going with you."

"If we both get shot, who's going for help? You stay here until I call for you or until something happens and I need you."

Abby didn't like it, but she nodded. Fargo walked into the corn. The sun made crazy dark shadows on the ground, but at first it was easy enough to see where Angel had passed by. Although the ground hadn't been plowed recently, it was soft enough for Angel to have left a light impression on it. Fargo followed her tracks, being careful to keep an eye out for her. He didn't think she could have gotten too far, and he thought she might be waiting for him. And she had Abby's pistol.

After going about halfway through the field, Fargo saw that Angel's tracks were much fainter, almost disappearing completely. He wondered why, and then realized that she must have been even weaker than he'd thought. After the excitement of escaping, she'd tired quickly, and now she was probably just ahead of him.

But she wasn't. Fargo looked all around; he couldn't find her. It took him a minute or two to locate more tracks, and then he knew he'd been tricked. Angel had slipped over to another row, turned around, and gone the other way. She'd passed him by and was headed back to the house.

Fargo didn't know why she was going there, but he knew it couldn't be for any good reason. Good, that is, from Fargo's point of view. He turned back and started to run, not minding that he was brushing against the cornstalks and making as much noise as a buffalo herd.

When he pushed aside the last green stalks and emerged from the field, Angel was there, all right. She was standing behind Abby, holding the pistol against the base of the smaller woman's skull.

When she saw Fargo, Angel said, "I'm glad it's you who came back. I knew I couldn't get back to my pa, but I thought I might get back at you some other way. I was willing to wait for however long it took until somebody showed up, but you came quicker than I even hoped."

Fargo had never liked to be tricked, but he had to admit that Angel had gotten the better of him. He said, "Now that you've fooled me, what are you going to do about it?"

"I'm going to kill this dainty little trollop," Angel said. "It's too bad her father's not here to see it, but you're just as good. You're the one that held me like this in front of my own father. Now you can feel a little of what he did. And this whore can feel what I felt."

"I'm not a whore," Abby said. "And I'm not afraid of you, either."

"Well, you should be. Because I'm just about to shoot the back of your head off."

"You don't want to do that, Angel," Fargo said. "It wouldn't be smart."

"I don't give much of a damn whether it's smart or not. In a way she's the one who got Paul killed, and it's only right that she's the one to pay for it."

That was just like the Murrays, Fargo thought, always looking for someone to blame.

"If Paul had stayed away from here, he'd still be alive," Fargo said. "Who's fault is it that he came?"

"Don't start that kind of talk with me," Angel said. "I'm going to shoot this bitch."

"If you do, I'll kill you," Fargo said.

"What do I care? You're just using me against my father, and we Murrays don't like to be used."

"You talk too much," Abby said. "And you're standing too close."

She raised her foot and stomped down on Angel's instep.

Angel yelped. Abby whirled around and smacked her in the face with a tiny fist. Angel stumbled back a step, and Abby struck at her again. She missed. Angel brought up the pistol, but she didn't get a chance to pull the trigger.

Abby slammed headfirst into her midsection, and both women hit the ground, Abby on top. Angel struck at Abby's head with the pistol, but she didn't seem to do much damage. Abby raised her fist and clubbed her in the wounded shoulder. Angel let out a yell to rival the ones Fargo had heard from Molly not too long ago under entirely different circumstances.

By the time the scream had died, Fargo was beside the two struggling women. Angel was trying to head-butt Abby, but the smaller woman had pulled back and was preparing to hit Angel's shoulder again.

Fargo bent over and grabbed Abby's wrist with one hand to restrain her while he wrested the pistol from Angel with his other hand.

"That's enough," he said to Abby. "I think you've got her whipped."

"The hell she does," Angel said. "You get away from her and let us fight. I'll tear her head off."

Fargo didn't think so. Abby had proved to be a lot less delicate than Molly seemed to think she was. Abby might be small, but she was a fighter.

Fargo kept his grip on her wrist and eased her up off Angel. Abby couldn't resist one last kick at Angel's ribs as Fargo pulled her away.

"Bitch," Angel said. She struggled to sit up. "Let her go, Fargo. I'm going to kill her."

"Looks to me like you're the one getting killed," Fargo said. "You should have shot her back in the house when you had the chance."

"I wanted someone to see and suffer the way my father did when you put the gun to my head. You bastard. This is all your fault."

Fargo wondered why people like Angel, and her father for that matter, always had to blame someone else for their troubles. They never seemed to think that any blame should light on them, no matter what they'd done.

"You might as well get up," Fargo said. "You seem to be feeling pretty feisty."

"That's what you think," Angel said, and then she fainted.

"That's the second time she's done that," Fargo said. "I don't think she's feeling too well after all."

"That's just fine with me," Abby said. "I don't care if

she dies. I hope she does. And you can let go of my arm. I'm not going to do anything else to her."

"I think you've done enough, already. Let's get her back in the house."

"Why don't we just leave her here? Let her lie there and die. I hate her."

"She doesn't think too much of you, either, judging by those names she called you. But it wouldn't be smart to let her die. I made a promise to Murray, and I'm going to keep it."

"Even after what she did?"

"What she did doesn't matter. She didn't make any promises."

"You sound a lot like Jed sometimes," Abby said. "I didn't understand him, either."

She turned and started back to the house. Then she remembered her pistol and came back for it. When she picked it up, she said, "You can bring her in if you want to, but don't expect me to help you."

"You'll have to watch her," Fargo said.

"If you want her watched, you do it. I don't think she's going anywhere."

Fargo picked up Angel and carried her back to the house. She didn't stir until he put her on the bed, and even then she didn't awaken. Abby was right. Angel wasn't going anywhere, not for a while.

Fargo sat down in the chair across from the bed. He removed his Colt from the holster and put it under his leg just in case Angel was faking. She wouldn't be able to get to the pistol without waking him up. When he was as comfortable as he could get, he closed his eyes, and in less than a minute he was asleep.

He woke up when he heard voices in another room. Angel was awake, too, and watching him, but she wasn't saying anything.

For the first time Fargo noticed that she was a beautiful woman, or would have been if not for the perpetual scowl she wore. Her hair was long and dark, her eyes were a startling blue, and her mouth was wide and sensuous. Fargo already knew she had an inviting figure from his earliest encounter with her in the barn. It was too bad that she was

76

an outlaw's daughter and that she'd chosen to follow her father's way of life.

Fargo grinned at her and said, "I thought you'd sleep a lot longer."

"I've been thinking about what's going to happen to you when my pa gets through with you," Angel said. "You won't be much of a man after he finishes cutting."

"I don't plan to give him a chance to start, much less finish."

"That shows how much you know about it. He runs things around here, and you just haven't figured it out yet."

"The way Jed hadn't?"

"I don't want to talk about him."

"Why not? You liked him for a while, or so I hear."

"He could have had everything, but he let his conscience get in the way. He deserved what happened to him."

She said the word *conscience* as if it were a curse. And the venom was still in her voice when she talked about Jed's fate. Fargo didn't agree with her conclusion, but he didn't feel like arguing with her. He put his pistol back in the holster and went out to see who was talking to Abby.

It was Lem, back from Johnson's place, and he was telling Abby a little about what had gone on there. Fargo hadn't told her because he hadn't had time. They'd been too concerned with catching up with Angel, and after that he'd been too tired.

"So there's not going to be a funeral for Sarah?" Abby said when Fargo walked into the kitchen.

"Just a little graveside ceremony for Rip and a couple of her women friends. There won't be any sitting up with her, either. Everybody's going to stay close to home for a few days. Some of them are even starting to talk about forming some kind of vigilance committee and doing something about Murray and that gang of his."

"You might not want to say that too loud," Fargo said, with a glance back over his shoulder.

"I don't care if she hears," Lem said. "Those Murrays find out everything sooner or later, anyhow. They've had things their own way around here for long enough. It's time somebody did something about them."

"That's the kind of talk that got Jed killed," Abby said. "I don't want to lose you, too."

"They won't kill me. I'm too old and ornery."

"They'll kill anybody. They killed Sarah Johnson."

"I blame Rip for that," Lem said. "He's pretending to be all torn up about it. But I know how he was around women. He might be just as glad she's gone."

As he said that last part, Fargo waited for Abby's reaction. She didn't mince words.

"He doesn't care one bit about Sarah. He'll be making a play for some other woman before she's cold in the ground."

"I know who that woman will be," Lem said, "and so do you. I don't like it."

"I don't like it any better than you do," Abby told him. "But if he thinks he's got a chance with me, he's got another thing coming. He'd better not even come around here."

"You know he likes you. He always has. He won't stay away."

"He doesn't like me any more than he likes any other woman. Which I admit is probably quite a lot. What he'd really like to do is get this farm for himself. But you don't have to worry about that. He doesn't have a chance with me."

"I thought you felt that way," Lem said, "But I'm glad to hear you say it. He'd make a mighty sorry son-in-law."

Fargo looked out the window and judged from the sunlight that it must be sometime past noon. He'd slept longer than he thought. And he realized that he was hungry. When he said something about it, Lem told Abby to fry up some bacon and eggs.

"I guess none of us have had any breakfast today. What about Angel?"

"She can wait," Abby said.

The bacon smelled good while it was frying in the pan, and it tasted even better than it smelled. The fresh eggs were just as tasty, and Fargo, for just a second or two, could almost understand why someone might want to settle down to the farming life. But only for a second or two. Being stuck in one place, living day after day under the same roof, seeing the same people all the time: those things didn't have any appeal for Fargo, and he was already getting anxious to get away from Kansas and back to some country where there were mountains with the snow still on top and streams that rushed down their sides instead of sliding along the flatlands.

While they were eating, Fargo asked Lem about the Murray gang, trying to find out a little more about them.

"Murray just showed up here one day a couple of years ago," Lem said. "Nobody knows much about him, but I doubt that he got his start here. I think he came because things are so unsettled hereabouts. He could run that gang of his without too much interference, and that's the way he wants it."

"And nobody tries to stop them?" Fargo asked.

"They take whatever they want, whenever they feel like it," Lem said around a mouthful of eggs. "They steal our chickens to eat, but they kill the rest of them for fun. They live off us, is what they do. We work, and they take what they please because we can't stop them."

"We could stop them if we did what Jed suggested," Abby said.

"It's hard to get farmers to turn to the gun," Lem said. "That's why they're farmers. They might talk about doing something, but they never do. Hell, I should know. I'm one of 'em."

"What about the town?" Fargo asked. "Does Murray ever go there?"

"Atchison? Sure, he goes there. He's robbed the bank there at least twice, but the sheriff's afraid of him. He might get together a posse, but they never seem to be able to find Murray. Pretty sorry posse, if you ask me."

That fit with what Molly had already told Fargo, and the thought of Molly made him wonder where she was.

"She's decided to stay at Talley's," Lem said when Fargo asked. "There's nobody else to do it, and she doesn't have a place anymore. The bank probably owns it now, but Molly might be able to take it over and pay off Talley's loan. 'Course, it wouldn't be easy, paying hers and his, too, but if anybody can do it, Molly can. She's a worker."

"Maybe she and Rip could partner up," Fargo said, just to see what Lem thought.

But it was Abby who answered as soon as she could quit laughing.

"Molly and Rip? You must be crazy, Fargo. Molly likes that man even less than I do, which is saying a lot."

Fargo knew that was true, and he decided it was time to bring the talk back to Murray.

"Why is it that nobody seems to know where the gang stays when they're not out raiding the countryside?" he asked. "Hasn't anybody tried to find them?"

"Not very hard," Lem said. "Fella named Melton tried once. We found him a day or so later, hanging in a tree at the end of a rope with his neck all stretched out. That pretty much discouraged people from looking."

Fargo could see how it would discourage the farmers, but it didn't bother him. He'd seen worse. Maybe he'd have a look around and see what he could find. Or maybe there was another way.

"We need to take good care of Angel," he said. "Keep her in bed another day or so and then send her on her way."

"We can't be rid of her soon enough for me," Abby said, and she crunched a bite of bacon between her teeth as if she were snapping a bone.

11

Two days passed without any real excitement, which was all right with Fargo. He needed the rest.

Sarah Johnson was buried quietly and without incident, and on the very afternoon of her burial, Rip showed up at Lem's house, asking for Lem.

Fargo didn't hear what the two of them talked about, but Abby told him later that Rip had asked her father for permission to come courting her.

"Can you believe the gall of that man?" she said. "His wife hasn't been in the grave more than an hour. She's hardly cold in the ground, and he shows up here' asking to come around to badger me."

"He didn't say he wanted to *badger* you, did he?" Fargo said.

"It doesn't matter what he said. It comes down to the same thing."

Fargo knew it wasn't funny, but he couldn't help grinning.

"What did Lem tell him?"

"He told him that it was indecent to talk about any such of a thing until his wife had been dead for at least six months."

"How did Rip take it?"

"You'd think he'd have been ashamed, but not him. You couldn't shame him if you tried. He said that out here a man needs a wife and that he couldn't afford to wait. He and his wife never had any family, and he wanted to have some children to help out on the farm." Abby shuddered. "I don't want to think about him touching me, much less doing anything else."

"Maybe in six months he'll have found himself somebody else."

"He better have. He's never getting his hands on me, I can tell him that."

The way she said it, and the fierce look on her face, convinced Fargo that she meant every word of it.

Tom Talley was buried even more quietly than Sarah Johnson had been. None of the farmers wanted to leave their homes and property long enough for a proper funeral, so hardly anyone was there to hear the preacher say a few words and a prayer.

Molly Doyle was part of the small group at both funerals, as was Fargo. Molly told Fargo that she came because she liked both people, and, after all, she didn't have a house to protect, unless she counted Talley's. She figured that one wasn't hers quite yet, though she told Fargo she was making some progress with the bank. She thought she would be the new owner within a few days.

Fargo went to the funerals because he thought there was a chance Murray might show up and try to get a little more revenge. But it didn't happen, and Fargo hoped that Murray had given up harassing the farmers. He knew, however, that most likely wasn't the case. Murray was probably waiting for the release of his daughter before becoming active again.

As for Angel, she improved rapidly. Her shoulder would have healed even faster if Abby hadn't pounded on it during their scuffle, but even with that extra bit of stress, it did just fine. The wound would leave a scar, but only a small one, and Angel was feeling fine. There was really no reason to keep her at the Watkins place any longer. She had served her purpose, and Fargo wanted to keep his end of the bargain by letting her go back to her father.

"You know that if she goes back to that marauder, he'll be right back up to his old tricks again," Lem said. "We ought to keep her here as long as we can."

"We ought to do worse than that," Abby said, looking entirely too bloodthirsty to suit Fargo.

"If she stays here, someone will have to watch her all the time," Fargo pointed out. "She's already gotten away from us once, so we might even have to tie her up. And you'll have to feed her. I don't see the sense in going to all the trouble and expense."

He had something else in mind, too, but he didn't want to mention it.

"Sooner or later, you're going to have to let her go, I guess," Lem said.

It was clear that neither he nor Abby was fond of the idea, but they had to admit that they weren't any fonder of having to keep Angel in the house for much longer.

"Murray might get it in his head to come after her," Lem said. "And that wouldn't be any good. No telling what kind of damage he'd do to this place if he got her away from us. Look at what he did to Molly's."

"We should go after him first," Abby said. "Root him out of wherever it is he's hiding, and take care of him and his whole gang once and for all."

For a day or so, Fargo had thought the farmers might actually band together. There was some talk of it, but it died down without any action being taken. Lem had been right. If they'd been fighters, they wouldn't have chosen farming as a way to make a living.

"No chance of this bunch around here getting organized against Murray," Lem said. "No matter how bad things get."

"Maybe when Angel goes back, he'll move somewhere else," Fargo said.

Lem shook his head. "No chance of that, either. He knows he has us cowed. Why take a chance on a new herd?"

Fargo didn't have any answer for that one. He said, "Angel has to leave anyway. I'll go tell her."

He pushed his chair back from the kitchen table where they were sitting and went in to talk to Angel.

She didn't appear entirely unhappy to see him. For the last day or so, there had been something like interest in her eyes every time Fargo entered the room. He wasn't quite sure why, but he had a feeling that she wasn't used to having a man treat her as a woman instead of just another member of the gang.

From what Fargo knew of him, Murray didn't seem to be the kind of man who'd take it kindly if one of his hirelings showed any interest in Angel, so it might be that she didn't often have a man paying any attention to her at all, for fear that Murray might cut off his ears, or some other vital part of his anatomy. Fargo thought that maybe Jed was the last man who'd had anything to do with her. Jed wouldn't have been afraid of Murray.

"I think it's about time you were going back to your father," Fargo said, standing in the doorway and looking at Angel, who was sitting up in the soft bed with several pillows at her back.

The light came in through the window and shone on her hair, which seemed even blacker because of it. Her blue eyes glowed. She was wearing one of Abby's cotton gowns, which was much too small for her and failed to do much to conceal the bounty of her breasts. Fargo could see the firm nipples pressing against the tight fabric. He didn't look away, and Angel didn't seem to mind.

"Are you sure you want me to leave?" she asked him.

Fargo raised his eyes to hers, and he could see that she was amused. There wasn't much doubt she knew the effect her appearance was having on him.

I think it would be best for everybody around here," Fargo said. "Your father wants you back, and I told him we'd let you leave when you were ready. You are ready, aren't you?"

"I'm always ready," Angel said.

Fargo wasn't quite sure how to respond to that, though he was almost certain she didn't exactly mean she was ready to go back to Murray.

Angel smoothed the front of the gown with her hands, running them over her breasts and tightening the fabric even more. Fargo thought that her breasts would burst right on through if she wasn't careful. But maybe that was what she wanted. He knew damn well he wouldn't mind.

"What about you, Fargo?" she said. "Are you ready?"

"As ready as any man you'll ever meet," Fargo said, deciding to join in the game.

Angel looked directly at his crotch, where he could feel his manhood thickening and stirring around.

"I can see you're not lying to me," she said. "I like a man who's not afraid to tell the truth."

"Well, then, I'll tell you some more. The truth is that you can't stay here anymore. Lem can't afford to keep feeding you, and I'm tired of sleeping in the barn."

84

"I'd think somebody in the house might offer to share a bed with you."

In fact, Abby had made the offer, but Fargo had turned her down. It was too risky to fool around with Lem in the house, and sober to boot. Fargo had considered paying Molly a visit at Talley's place, but that hadn't seemed like such a good idea, either.

"Lem offered, but I think he snores," Fargo said. "I can't tolerate a man who snores."

"Do you snore, Fargo?"

"Not that I know of, but then I'm a sound sleeper. You'll have to find out about the snoring for yourself."

"I might do that one of these days. But not right now. Right now, I guess you want me to get dressed."

"That's the idea. But first I thought you might want to show your gratitude for being taken care of so well."

"How did you think I'd go about doing that?"

"You could thank Lem and Abby for giving you a bed and for changing your bandages. And for feeding you."

Angel stopped smiling. "I'm not thanking anybody. I wouldn't have to be taken care of if you hadn't shot me."

"I only did that because I had to," Fargo said. "You would have done the same if you found yourself in that situation."

"I don't think so. I'd have fought it out."

"And gotten killed? I don't think so. There's a time and a season for everything, a time for fighting and a time for saving your life."

"That sounds like something from the Bible."

"That's not from the Bible. It's from the Book of Fargo, chapter three, verse four."

"No matter where it's from, I have to admit, I'm kind of glad you didn't get killed."

"Why do you say that?"

"If you're lucky, you might find out someday." Angel shoved the covers off. "Now if you'll get out of here, I'll put my clothes on."

"I might as well stay," Fargo said. "I don't want you to escape."

"You're letting me go, remember? You just want to get a look at something you're not going to see. You're not that lucky, Fargo. Not today. Now get out of here before I raise a ruckus."

Fargo didn't want that, so he moved out of the doorway.

"And close the door," Angel said.

Fargo did, but he was sorry he had to.

After Angel was dressed, Abby gave her some lunch. Neither woman spoke to the other while Angel ate, and Fargo stayed out of the way.

When Angel had eaten, Fargo went with her to the barn to help saddle her horse. Her arm still wasn't strong enough for a job like that, no matter how nicely it was healing.

When the horse was saddled, Angel managed to swing herself up on its back without any help from Fargo, who didn't even offer. She didn't look as if she would have appreciated it.

She settled herself in the saddle and said, "You're not going to try to follow me, are you?"

"Never even gave it a thought," Fargo lied.

It had been his plan from the beginning to follow her back to her father's hiding place. He had promised to take care of her, but he hadn't promised anything else.

"You couldn't do it anyway," she said. "So I'm not worried about it. Too much open country around here. I could see you a long way off."

Fargo knew that well enough. But Angel didn't know about his tracking abilities. He could trail her from so far back that she'd never know he was there. And if he could discover Murray's whereabouts, it was possible he could talk the farmers into getting together and mounting a sneak attack. It would be one way to pay Murray back for Jed.

Maybe that thought didn't make Fargo any better than Murray, but at least Fargo didn't spend his time preying on other people.

"I'll be on my way, then," Angel said. "It's too bad we didn't meet a different way, Fargo. It might have been interesting."

"It could still be interesting," Fargo said. "You don't have to live the way you do."

"That's what Jed thought. But he was wrong, and you see what happened to him."

"I've been wondering about that," Fargo said, but Angel wouldn't let him continue.

"It doesn't pay to wonder," she said. "A man can get in a lot of trouble that way, and I don't want to make any more trouble for you. You're in enough trouble already."

Fargo didn't have to ask what she meant by that. He had a feeling that Murray might be after him again as soon as Angel was safe. Angel went on to confirm that he was right.

"Pa blames you for what happened to Paul," she said. "It's not just that you killed him. You put him in that shallow hole and called it a burying."

"He wouldn't have been killed or buried, either, if he'd stayed away from here."

"That's not the way we Murrays look at things."

Angel turned the horse's head and started to ride away. After the horse had gone a few paces, she pulled up on the reins and looked back over her shoulder.

"If you were smart," she said, "you'd get back to wherever it is you came from and leave these farmers to us."

"I never was too smart," Fargo said. "Not smart enough to run out on my friends, anyhow."

"Too bad. But at least I tried to warn you. I guess you just like trouble too much."

"I don't like trouble. It just seems to come my way now and then."

"It wouldn't if you'd mind your own business."

"Maybe I'm just too curious."

"You know what they say about curiosity and the cat?"

"I've heard about it," Fargo said. "Can't say as I ever believed it, though. Cats have nine lives, after all."

"And I don't believe that," Angel said. "So long, Fargo."

She turned and snapped the reins. The horse started off at a walk, but before she'd gone too far, she urged it to go faster. She was such a good rider that she didn't bounce enough to bother her shoulder.

Fargo watched her until she was almost out of sight. Then he saddled the Ovaro and went after her.

Fargo had no trouble at all following the tracks of Angel's horse. It was almost as if she wanted to be followed, he thought, so he was wary of a trap. Not that there was any place to trap him.

He rode across fields, past cornfields and farmhouses, always staying so far back that there was no chance of

Angel catching a glimpse of him. She didn't seem to be in any particular hurry, so Fargo dawdled along as slowly as he could.

It wasn't long before he knew where Angel was headed. She was riding right toward the creek, and she would enter the trees that grew along it not far from the spot where her brother had first been buried. If she got into the trees, she might have a better chance of losing him, but Fargo didn't think she would. He could track her there as easily as he could out in the open.

But Angel was taking no chances, as Fargo learned when he reached the creek bank. The sun came through the tree limbs and sketched shadows on the ground. The water in the creek was shallow and slow-moving, and Angel had ridden right into it.

It didn't take Fargo long to discover that she hadn't ridden out on the other side.

He sat on the Ovaro for a minute and thought about it. He had only two choices, left or right. He could take one direction for a while and then the other. It shouldn't take him too long to find out where she'd left the stream, unless she hadn't left it at all. If she hadn't, she might lose him if he didn't make the right choice.

He turned the horse's head to the right. Might as well try in that direction first, he thought. The trees grew close to the water in places, and there might be some sign of her passing. If there wasn't, he'd go back and try the other way.

After he'd gone a couple of hundred yards down the narrow, winding waterway, the banks grew steeper on either side of him, and the trees grew more thickly. It wouldn't have been easy to ride a horse up the muddy banks, and Fargo was beginning to think it was time to turn around and go back the other way. But then he saw up ahead of him a cut in the bank, begun when water from some heavy rain in the past had found a crack in the earth and rushed into the creek, leaving a track for water to flow through later.

Fargo rode up to the cut and saw the tracks of Angel's horse leading up the bank. He turned the Ovaro's head and followed the tracks.

He didn't have far to go.

In the trees a few yards ahead, Angel was waiting for him.

12

Her horse's reins were tied to a tree limb, and Angel stood there, her hands on her hips. She was wearing only her shirt, and it hung down just far enough to cover the part of her body that Fargo automatically looked for. Her legs were slim and white, tapering to trim ankles. The sunlight fell through the leaves and dappled her dark hair.

"I thought maybe I'd lost you," she said.

"That's not as easy to do as you think," Fargo told her, halting the Ovaro. "Aren't you afraid you might get the grippe, dressed like that?"

Angel gave him a languorous smile and said, "You mean undressed, don't you?"

"I guess I do."

"The weather's still warm. I don't think I'll get sick. Why don't you get down off that horse so we can talk. I don't like looking up at you. It hurts my neck."

Fargo slid off the Ovaro, led it over to a nearby tree, and looped the reins over a branch.

"I knew you'd follow me," Angel said. "So I thought I'd come somewhere we could have a little privacy."

Fargo looked around. They were in a little clearing in the trees, with the only real opening being the narrow cut that he'd just ridden out of. He could hear some birds in the trees, and a squirrel chattered away somewhere nearby. But there was nothing else to hear, not even the sluggish flow of the creek. Fargo didn't think there was much danger that anyone would find them there.

"You picked a good spot," he said. "What did you have in mind?"

For an answer Angel started to unbutton the shirt. She

took her time about it, letting Fargo wonder a while about what he was going to see, but eventually she got it done. The shirt hung loosely on her, but she'd been careful not to let it gape open. Fargo could still see no more than he'd seen when he first arrived.

Angel smiled. "You remember what I said when you asked me if I was ready?"

Fargo nodded. "You said you were always ready."

"That's right, and now you're about to find out just how ready I am."

She took both hands and opened the shirt, holding it wide.

Fargo saw that her breasts were even bigger than he'd thought, standing high and proud, with their erect nipples pointing straight at him like bullets. Her waist was small enough for him to circle with his two hands and emphasized the curve of her hips. The crisp hair on her mound was as black as the hair on her head, and it was thickly tangled. The puckered red wound in her shoulder didn't detract from her beauty at all.

"The question is," Angel said, "are you ready, Fargo?"

"I'm as ready as anybody ever was," Fargo said, which was the truth if he'd ever told it.

Angel let the shirt fall to the ground and walked to where a nearby tree shaded a pile of leaves that Fargo thought she must have gathered there while waiting for him to catch up with her. She lay down on the leaves, careful not to hurt her shoulder, and let his eyes take her in. As he watched, she spread her legs and let her fingers play with her dense pubic hair for a moment before allowing her middle finger to slip into the enticing crack between her legs. She let the finger remain motionless for a second or two before rubbing herself lightly. Her hips wiggled, her lips parted, and she moaned deep in her throat, letting her finger slip inside herself.

"What the hell are you waiting for, Fargo?" she said huskily after a moment had passed. "I don't want to have to do this all by myself."

Fargo didn't want her to have to, but it occurred to him that she might have led him into some kind of trap. He didn't see how that could be, though. She didn't have a gun unless she'd found one hidden in the trees, which seemed highly doubtful. And there was no one else within miles as

90

far as Fargo could tell. Just the birds and squirrel, and not even the squirrel was silent. Fargo shucked his clothes off as quickly as he could and joined her on the leaves.

She immediately moved her hand from herself to his erection, which was already standing at attention like a soldier on parade. Her fingers were wet and slick from the caresses she'd given herself. She slid them up and down the length of Fargo's iron-hard shaft.

"You could use that for a club if you got in a brawl," Angel said.

"It might not be as much like a club if I were in a fight," Fargo said. "It needs a little encouragement."

"Why don't I give it some, then?"

Angel turned over on him and took him in her mouth. Its soft wet heat engulfed him, and she teased the tip of his pole with her tongue before taking him deeper and deeper. He looked at her through hooded eyes and saw that she had her hand busy between her legs.

"I can take care of that job for you," he said, taking her hips in his hands and positioning her so that he could get to her dripping honey pot with his mouth and tongue. He let his tongue glide over her, and she shuddered in pleasure. He kept it up for a while and then quickly slipped his tongue into her. As soon as he did it, she jerked as if she'd been shot.

"Ohhhhhhhhhh!" she said. "My sweet Jesus! Ohhhhhhhhh!"

She collapsed on him and lay there for a while, breathing heavily. Finally she rose and got off him, lying back on the leaves.

"I wasn't expecting that," Angel said. "Good Lord!"

Fargo didn't say anything.

"It didn't do you much good did it?" Angel said. She reached for him with her hand and found him as hard as ever. "When you say you're ready, you really do mean it. I'm sorry it's all over."

"What do you mean?"

"Well, I've, you know . . . finished. I didn't mean for it to happen like that, but it's too late to do anything about it now."

She hadn't had as much experience as Fargo thought she had. Either that, or the men she'd known hadn't had much stamina. The fact that she'd finished only once was hardly a drawback to what was about to happen. Fargo was a little disappointed in Jed for just a second, but then he forgot all about him.

"You haven't finished," Fargo said. "You just think you have. I'll show you."

He started by kissing her breasts, then flicking the nipples with his tongue before taking each one into his mouth in its turn. To what seemed like Angel's surprise, her nipples grew hot and hard again, and her breasts engorged. Fargo let his own fingers get to work doing what Angel's had been doing earlier. She moaned and sighed, and her hips wiggled on the bed of leaves that rustled beneath her.

Fargo rose up and parted her legs, positioning himself between them. His rampant erection jutted out in front of him like a spear, and Angel took it in both hands.

"You were right, Fargo. It's not too late. This is what I need, and I need it now. Give it to me!"

Fargo needed no further invitation. Being careful of her shoulder, he buried himself in her right up to the limit.

"Ahhhhhhh!" Angel said, her head twisting to the side, her mouth wide and wanton.

Fargo held her pinned there for a while before starting to move. When he slid out, he went back in almost immediately. It was as if Angel had somehow pulled him back inside, and his strokes became faster and faster, with Angel thrashing beneath him as if she were having some kind of seizure.

Fargo was just at the point of explosion when Angel suddenly became still. He thought for an instant that he might have hurt her shoulder, but it wasn't that. It was only the calm before the tornado struck. She bucked under him like an unbroken pony. She bounced him, jounced him, and nearly threw him off. And then she climaxed.

"Ahhhhhhh! Ahhhhhh! Ahhhhhh!"

Soon Fargo joined her. He felt entirely drained, and Angel couldn't say a thing. They lay side by side and waited until their hearts stopped trying to beat through their chests.

After several minutes, Angel said, "It's too bad you're the kind of man you are, Fargo."

"What kind of man is that?"

"The same kind that Jed was. Well, you're certainly different in one way. But I'm not talking about that. He was stiff-necked and honest, and it got him killed."

"There's nothing wrong with being honest," Fargo said. "It's the way most people are."

"Not my people. We haven't been that way for a long time. Not since my mother was killed."

"What happened to her?"

"It happened a few years ago. My pa was a farmer, just like all these people around here. He probably would have stayed one if it hadn't been for the free-staters and the slavery crowd."

Fargo wondered what that had to do with anything, but he figured if he waited, Angel would tell him.

"My pa was like these farmers you're staying with," she went on. "He didn't care one way or the other about slavery or what happened to other people. He just wanted to be left alone to get his crops in and take care of me and Paul and our mother."

She didn't look at Fargo when she mentioned Paul's name. She was probably thinking about how he had died.

"One day, my mother went to town. Alice. Her name was Alice, but I never called her that. There was a fight there that day between the free-staters and some of the people who favored slavery. She got caught in the middle, for no reason. She was just there. But she got killed anyway."

"I'm sorry about that," Fargo said, meaning it. "But I don't see what it has to do with your father's war against the farmers here. Looks like his quarrel is with somebody else."

"That's not the way he sees it. He thinks people should have done something about my mother, but nobody ever did. She was just in the way, they said, and it wasn't anybody's fault that she died. That was the way people looked at it. Pa tried to do something, but nobody listened to him. He came home one night and told me and Paul that he was going to make people sorry they'd ever messed with the Murray family. He was going to get revenge on the ones responsible, and on everybody else besides. Nobody was ever going to cross the Murrays again. The world belonged to the strong and the violent, he said, and he was going to be as strong and as violent as anybody in it."

"That's not going to do a lot of good for your mother," Fargo said.

"No, it's not." Angel sat up and then got to her feet. "It seems to do a lot for Pa, though, and Paul understood. Now Paul's gone, and somebody's going to have to pay for that."

Fargo stood beside her. He thought he might as well try to explain things to her one more time, for all the good it would do.

"It was as much your father's fault that Paul died as it was anybody's," he said. "If you hadn't been out to get revenge on Jed, both of them would be alive, and quite a few others would, too. Sarah Johnson. Tom Talley. Just to name a couple of them."

"You don't understand," Angel said. She began getting into her clothes. "There's more to it than I've told you."

Fargo started to get dressed as well. When he was finished, he said, "Why don't you tell me what else there is about what's going on around here."

"That's not for me to do. I'm not even sure I know exactly what it is. Pa doesn't tell me everything, the way he did Paul. You've been fun, Fargo, but I have to keep some of my secrets, even though you've treated me better than any man ever has, even Jed. You know a few tricks he didn't, and I appreciate it."

"I'd say the pleasure was all mine," Fargo told her, "but you and I both know better."

Angel blushed and then smiled. "I guess we do, at that. I'm sorry it has to stop, but we won't be seeing each other again. Not like this."

She went over to her horse and untied the reins from the limb. Then she managed to get in the saddle again without Fargo's help.

"I'm going to ask you a favor, Fargo. I know you're a man of your word, so I'm going to ask you not to follow me. I think you owe me that."

"All right," Fargo said. "I won't follow you."

"Thank you for that. I don't want to see you get killed, not this soon after we, well, you know."

"That's mighty nice of you," Fargo said. "I don't want to get killed at all."

"Then mind your own business and maybe you won't," Angel said, and rode off through the trees.

Fargo watched her go, and when she was out of sight, he got up on the Ovaro and went back to the Watkins farm. He thought about Angel and what she had said all the way.

13

The Murray gang struck at Alf Wesley's farm that night around midnight. Wesley was asleep when the shooting started, but he must have run outside and tried to put a stop to it.

He didn't have a chance. He was shot to ribbons before he got off his front porch.

The Murrays stayed around after he was dead, shooting and hollering and generally having themselves a fine old time. It was as if they were trying to attract attention to what they'd done, and if attention was what they wanted, they got it. Wesley farm was close enough to Lem's for the noise to awaken Fargo, and it didn't take him long to get the Ovaro saddled and go to see what the trouble was.

Lem wanted to go with him, but Fargo told him to stay at home.

"You can't leave Abby here alone," the Trailsman said. "And we don't want her to go with us. You need to be here to put up some kind of fight if they come this way. Make plenty of noise if anybody shows up here, and I'll come back."

Lem said that he'd try to make as much noise as he could, but Fargo could see that he wasn't happy about staying.

"You think they've killed Alf?" Lem asked.

"That's what I'm going to find out," Fargo said.

The gang didn't seem too worried that anyone would interfere with their fun. And they needn't have been. As Fargo neared Wesley's farm, he realized that no farmers had come in response to the ruckus, and he didn't think any of them would be coming along later, even though the shooting could be heard for miles. Everybody heard it, Fargo was sure, but nobody appeared willing to take the risk of leaving his own house.

Fargo didn't really blame them. They had their own homes and families to think of. On the other hand, Fargo couldn't understand why they wouldn't want to help out a neighbor, even though it would be a risk. Maybe that was another reason he'd never become a farmer.

He left the Ovaro on the far side of the cornfield and made his way through the tall rustling stalks. He didn't have to worry about making noise. The gang members were riding around the house and barn, brandishing torches, shooting their pistols into the air, and yelling as if they'd had plenty to drink before coming to raid Wesley's property. They weren't going to hear a man walking through a cornfield. They probably wouldn't have heard a buffalo stampede.

In the light of the moon and the flickering torches, Fargo could see Alf Wesley's body lying sprawled a few feet away from the front of his house. He wasn't moving, and Fargo didn't doubt that he was dead. A rifle lay a short distance from one outstretched hand.

Peter Murray sat astride his horse near the house and watched the frolic with the dignified air of a circuit-riding preacher. He was tall, broad-shouldered, and a little thick through the middle. He had a thick, bushy beard that was mostly black, though it was silvered by the moon. Fargo couldn't really see his eyes, but they glowed crimson in the reflected torchlight, and Fargo thought he could see the ghost of a smile through the wild tangle of beard.

Angel was near her father, but she didn't seem quite so pleased with what was going on. She wasn't smiling, and her shoulders slumped. That could have been a result of her wound, but Fargo thought it was the result of her disapproval. He chuckled to himself. He was getting soft if he thought Angel didn't endorse what was happening. She knew what was going to happen before she rode out with the gang.

Fargo was a little sorry she was there because he was about to do something that would hurt her more than the death of her brother. He was going to kill her father. He

96

didn't see anything else he could do. He couldn't fight the whole gang, which had grown back to its original size or larger already, so he'd deal with it the way he'd deal with a snake: cut off the head and hope the body would die. It was a little like bushwhacking, and Fargo didn't like it. However, Murray hadn't given Wesley much of a chance, either.

Fargo pulled his Colt from the holster and brought it up to shoot, but before he could pull the trigger, someone came riding up, firing a shotgun and shrieking like a gut-shot antelope.

It was Molly Doyle, the only farmer with the gumption to take a hand in things. Instead of sneaking up on the gang like Fargo, she'd apparently decided to shoot it out single-handedly. Maybe she thought that they'd believe she was crazy and that would scare them away. If that was her idea, it didn't work, but it did slow things down a little.

Not because anybody was afraid of her. Crazy or not, she was using a gun with a limited range and with only two shells in it, not the kind of ordnance to strike fear into the heart of anybody with even a little knowledge of firearms. Anybody who got nicked by the buckshot fired from a distance was going to be more peeved than hurt. Several of Murray's men stopped riding around in circles and sat watching to see what Molly would do next.

Not having hit anybody with her shotgun, Molly simply tossed it away from her and pulled her pistol. She did a little better with that, and Fargo was surprised to see her shoot one man out of the saddle.

Probably just luck, Fargo thought. It wasn't easy to shoot straight while you were riding full tilt on horseback.

When the man fell from his horse, Molly turned and rode toward the spot where Murray and Angel had been. But they were no longer there. As soon as Molly had come into view, they had ridden away, and Fargo didn't know where they had gone. All he knew was that Molly had spoiled his chance of killing Murray and that she wasn't likely to catch up with him and do the job herself.

All she was going to do was get herself killed.

Unless Fargo did something to help her out.

He ran out of the cornfield, firing his pistol. He didn't

think he'd hit anybody. He was just trying to create a momentary distraction, to do something that would turn the attention to him and away from Molly.

It worked. Murray's men started shooting at Fargo, who ran a zigzag trail toward Molly. Approaching her horse from behind, Fargo holstered his pistol. He made a running jump, placed his hands on the horse's rump, and propelled himself onto the horse's back behind Molly. The horse reared up in surprise, but Fargo held onto Molly's waist and didn't fall. Reaching around her ample body, he grabbed the reins from her hands and snapped them against the horse's neck. The horse had recovered from its shock at the sudden addition to its load, and it jumped forward at a run.

Instead of heading away from the house, Fargo ran the horse straight toward Murray's men, who were so surprised at his audacity that they forgot to shoot for a second or two. By the time they remembered, Fargo was right in the middle of them, and then past them.

"It's Murray!" Molly yelled, and Fargo looked over her shoulder to see the leader of the gang, with Angel still at his side, not far away.

Murray and Angel weren't running away. They were sitting on their horses, silhouetted against the night sky, waiting with drawn pistols for Fargo and Molly to get closer.

Molly got off a couple of shots, but then the hammer of her pistol clicked on an empty chamber.

"Damn!" she said.

With the gang coming up behind him and Murray waiting in front, Fargo didn't have much choice of where to go. He jerked on the reins, hoping to turn the horse to the right, but the animal was moving too fast and the footing wasn't certain. The next thing Fargo knew, he and Molly were flying through the air, asses over elbows, and then he hit the ground, hard, and didn't know anything for a long time.

When Fargo came to, he had no idea where he was. Total darkness surrounded him. He might as well have been tied up inside a heavy leather bag for all that he could see. He was in a sitting position, and there was something hard against his back, something that felt like a rock. His head throbbed as if he'd been kicked by a horse.

The thought of being kicked in the head brought back

the memory of his fall. He must have hit his head somehow. He was lucky that his neck wasn't broken. Maybe it had been. Maybe he was dead and in hell. He knew there were plenty of people who'd wished him there over the years. The place he was in now didn't seem hot enough for hell, though. In fact, it was a little cool, and the rock at Fargo's back seemed damp. He had a feeling there wouldn't be a lot of damp rocks in hell. He couldn't smell any brimstone, either, and there weren't any fires. There was nobody with hooves and a forked tail. There was nothing, in fact, but the blackness. And the silence. Fargo realized for the first time that he couldn't hear a thing.

Then he realized that he couldn't feel his hands.

Had he gone deaf?

Had someone cut off his hands?

He tried to move and found that he couldn't. His feet were tied together, and his arms were behind him. Probably tied at the wrists, tied so tightly that the circulation was cut off. Which was why he couldn't feel them. That wasn't good. It could lead to some serious problems later on.

"Anybody here?" Fargo said. His voice was a hoarse croak.

His voice echoed off stone walls, and a voice not far away said. "Just me."

"Molly?"

"That's right. Are you all right, Fargo? I thought for sure you were dead."

Fargo's head pounded and his shoulders had started to ache.

"I might be better off if I was. Do you know where we are?"

"Murray's hideout. Don't talk too loud or somebody will hear us."

Fargo didn't think he could talk loud even if he wanted to. His throat felt as if it might be full of sharp-edged stones.

"I was wondering where the hideout was," he said, his voice rasping. "But now that I'm in it, I still don't know where it is."

"It's a cave. We're in a little valley not far from the Missouri River. This cave was carved out a long time ago when the river first came this way, I guess."

Fargo tried to take that in. "How far from Wesley's farm are we?"

"A pretty good distance. You've been out for a long time."

Fargo thought about that. The inside of his mouth was dry and tasted like it had been stuffed with burned chicken feathers.

"Why didn't they just kill us?"

"They were going to at first. That's what Murray wanted to do, but Angel talked him out of it. She said something about you being different from the rest of the farmers, that maybe you'd throw in with them, but I don't think she fooled Murray much. He knew what she really meant." Molly chuckled. "You get around, don't you, Fargo."

Fargo didn't see any point in talking about that. He said, "What about you? They could have killed you."

"I guess they figured that if they were going to keep you around for a while, they might as well keep me, too. Or maybe Murray fancies me."

"I wouldn't blame him if he did," Fargo said.

"That's mighty gallant of you, Fargo, especially considering that we're trussed up like a pair of turkeys. But I don't really think Murray fancies me. I don't think they'll keep either one of us alive for very long."

As he got more accustomed to the dark, Fargo realized that the blackness wasn't quite as intense as he'd at first believed. There was a faint glow almost directly across from him. It wasn't much, but he knew that the cave must have several rooms. Murray's gang was in one where there was light from fire and torches, while Fargo and Molly had been stuck back in one of the other, darker rooms.

Fargo wiggled his arms, trying to stimulate the circulation in his hands. He didn't have any luck.

"Why did you come charging up to Wesley's house like that?" Fargo asked. "You're lucky you didn't get killed right then and there."

"I was just so damn mad," Molly said. "I thought that by the time I got there, everybody from all around would have come to help Alf out. But there was nobody. Well, except for you, and I didn't know you were around. It made me mad that nobody cared about Alf, and I guess I just lost my head. Now I'll probably lose it anyhow."

"Maybe not. Maybe we can get out of here."

"Sure. Any minute now Angel will come in and cut you loose because she likes you so much. Let me set you straight, Fargo. You're good, but you're not that good. Besides, even if she cut the ropes, you'd never get past Murray."

"I wasn't thinking about Angel. I thought maybe you could cut these ropes. If you don't, I'm going to lose my hands."

"I don't have a knife, and I don't think I can chew these ropes in two. If there was a rat around, maybe he could do it for you."

Fargo didn't much like rats, and he'd just as soon Molly hadn't mentioned them. But there weren't likely to be any rats in a cave. He said, "I carry a knife in my boot. If we can get it out, and if you can get hold of it, we can at least get loose. After that, we can see about getting away from here."

"A knife? Why didn't you say so sooner? How can we get to it?"

"Can you get over here?"

"I can sure as hell try."

Fargo heard a muffled flop as Molly fell over and then a scratchy scraping sound as she snaked her way across the floor on her stomach. Within a minute or two, he felt her head bump his leg.

"I'm here," she said. "Now what?"

"Now we see if we can get to the knife."

Fargo wasn't actually sure the knife was there. Whoever tied his feet together might have noticed it and taken it. But Fargo didn't think that would have happened. The knife had been overlooked before and had gotten him out of more than one scrape. He slid down the wall until he was lying on his back with his arms and hands beneath him. It was just as well he couldn't feel anything back there, he thought. He'd probably be screaming if he could.

He managed somehow to raise his legs until they were pointing just about straight up at the ceiling. The knife didn't fall out of the boot. There were two possible reasons: either someone had removed it, as he'd feared, or the ropes that held his feet were tied so tightly that the knife was stuck.

"Damn," Fargo said, and then he explained the problem to Molly.

"Kick your feet around," she said. "Maybe you can shake it loose. If it's there, which I wouldn't count on."

Fargo bent his knees and kicked straight up. Nothing happened. He tried it again, and he thought he felt something move inside the boot. He couldn't be sure because by now he couldn't feel his lower legs and feet much better than he could feel his hands. Whoever had tied him had certainly done a good job of it. Or a bad job, depending on your point of view.

Fargo kicked again. The knife fell out of the boot, but its scabbard stayed inside. The hilt of the knife hit Fargo squarely on the breastbone, sending a sharp pain through his chest. He clamped his teeth shut and didn't cry out. He thought it was a good thing he'd been struck by the hilt and not the point of the blade. The knife bounced off his chest and hit Molly's head before falling to the floor.

"Now all you have to do is get your hands on it," Fargo said. "I'd do it myself, but I can't feel a thing."

"My fingers feel like pieces of cordwood," Molly said. "But I'll see what I can do."

She got into a sitting position and fumbled around for the knife. While she was groping, Fargo squirmed back up against the wall to wait until Molly got hold of the knife, if she ever managed it.

It took a while, but finally Molly said, "I think I have it. Scoot over here, and let's see what I can do."

Fargo dug in with his heels and pulled himself across the floor. When his feet encountered something soft, Molly said, "That's me. Turn around and back up to me."

Fargo did his best, and eventually they were back to back.

"Now's the hard part," Molly said. "I think I have the knife with the sharp edge of the blade facing you. I can hold onto it, maybe, if you can move your arms up and down."

Fargo didn't know of any other way to do it. Not being able to feel his hands, he was probably going to get cut pretty badly, but it wouldn't matter if the ropes got cut as well.

"Can you feel where I am?" he asked.

"You're about right. Get to moving."

Fargo moved. It was slow work because the knife occasionally slipped from Molly's hands, and then she was forced to pick it up and get it back into position. Fargo didn't ask why the knife slipped away. It could have happened because Molly's fingers were too numb to hold it. Or it could have been that her hands were slick with his blood. If it was the latter, he didn't want to know about it.

After what seemed to be several hours, though it was more like ten minutes, the ropes parted and Fargo's arms separated. But he couldn't do anything to help Molly, not then. He had to wait until the circulation returned to his hands and fingers.

That took another few minutes, and they were mighty painful ones. It was as if someone had stuck Fargo's hands into a fire and then stuck red-hot needles into his hands. When he could finally flex his fingers, the pain ran all the way up his arms. He found that his hands were covered with blood, but he couldn't feel the cuts yet. That would come later, and he didn't let it worry him. He found the knife and cut his feet free. Then he cut the ropes that bound Molly.

She groaned a little when her circulation began to come back, but not enough to be heard by anyone in another part of the cave.

"Well, we're loose," she said when she could speak again. "What now? We can't just walk out of here."

"We don't have a lot of other choices," Fargo said. "But at least we don't have to go out the front way."

"Who says there's another way?"

"Nobody. Sometimes there is, sometimes there isn't. We'll just have to find out."

"You might not have noticed," Molly said, "but it's darker than the inside of a black cat at midnight in here. And if we start going farther back, it's just going to get darker."

Fargo couldn't argue with that. He said, "You can go out and face Murray if you want to. I figure you'd get about one step into the light before you got shot four or five times. I'd rather take my chances in the dark if there's another way out of here."

"So we feel our way along, is that it?"

Fargo nodded, then realized that Molly couldn't see him. He said, "That's it. We'll either find a way out or get stuck somewhere and starve."

"I could do with missing a few meals, but I don't much like the idea of starving. And what about the bats?"

Fargo didn't know anything about bats.

"They're not in this part of the cave," Molly told him, "but I heard Murray talking about them. They're in here somewhere, and I don't like the idea of running into them."

"Bats won't hurt you."

"They'll tangle up in your hair. I don't think I could stand that. I lost my hat when we fell, or I wouldn't be worried."

Women never ceased to amaze Fargo. Here was one who'd charged at Murray and his gang even though she was outnumbered fifteen or twenty to one, and she was worried about bats.

"Bats don't get in your hair," Fargo said. "That's just a tale some folks like to tell."

"How do you know?"

"I know. The only thing you have to worry about is that the floor under their roost will be mighty nasty."

"As long as they don't get in my hair, I don't care."

"Then let's see if we can find a way out of here," Fargo said.

14

Fargo stuck his knife back in his boot, and he and Molly limped to the back wall of the room, where they started feeling their way in opposite directions: Fargo to the right and Molly to the left. Judging from the glow that Fargo could see across from them, the room was a fairly large one, though that didn't mean there was another exit or that it would be large enough for them to squeeze through even if it existed. And if there was an exit from the room, it might not lead them out of the cave. It could just as easily lead them deeper underground and have no outlet. Still, Fargo figured the risk was worth it. The outcome of facing Murray without a weapon other than a knife was pretty much a certainty. At least this way there was a chance, no matter how small it was.

"I found something here," Molly said after Fargo had gone only a few feet. "It's not very big, though."

"It might not be the only way out," Fargo said. "Keep looking."

They looked, but neither of them found any other way out. They met at the opening Molly had located, and Fargo tried to gauge its size by running his hand around the edges.

"I can see why Murray didn't bother to put a guard on us," he said. "He didn't think we could get out through here even if we did get loose."

"Was he right?" Molly asked. "Usually I don't mind being big, but there are times when I wish I was as small as Abby. This is one of them."

Fargo judged that the opening, which started almost at the level of the floor, was at most a couple of feet high and not much wider. They could snake along through it if it didn't get any narrower. Maybe it would widen out. Maybe not. If it didn't, they'd be stuck. But it was the best chance they had.

"I'll go first," he said. "If it gets too tight, you can back out."

"Not if I'm stuck."

"You won't get stuck," Fargo said with more confidence than he felt. "If I can make it through, so can you. Or you can stay here. That's up to you."

Fargo lay down on the floor and scooted into the opening. His shoulders cleared the sides by only a few inches, and it was even darker in there than where he'd just been. The absence of light was total. God only knew what he was getting into. Somebody had told him once that it was better to face the devil you knew than to take a chance of facing the devil you didn't know. He'd always thought that was a pretty craven way of thinking, but right now he wasn't so sure that it wasn't good advice.

Too late to worry about that, though. He slithered along as best he could, keeping his head low so as not to hit it on the rock above him. He didn't think he could help yelling if he did, since his head was still as sore as if he'd been scalped.

After a few minutes, he stopped moving and listened. He could hear Molly scraping along behind him. He didn't say anything. He just moved on.

It wasn't long before he lost all track of time. All he knew was that there was rock above him and rock below him and darkness all around him. It was like being buried alive. Now and then something like that happened to people, if you were to believe the stories that you heard around the campfire.

He could hear Molly's breathing now. It was too fast, and too shallow. She was getting close to panicking, Fargo thought, and he didn't much blame her. They were too far into the tunnel to go back.

The floor of the tunnel seemed to be sloping downward, and Fargo didn't know if that was good or bad. Bad, he guessed. The way out seemed more likely to be up than down. On the other hand, there probably weren't any bats down there on the lower levels. He kept moving forward, pulling himself with his elbows and pushing with his toes.

After another couple of minutes, he thought that something seemed different, and he raised up carefully. Sure enough, the roof of the tunnel was higher. He could get on his hands and knees and crawl. Better yet, if he slouched over, he could even sit up.

"We have a little more room," he told Molly. "Time for a rest."

Molly didn't say anything. She was panting. She sounded like a dog after a long run.

"We'll be fine," Fargo said, not knowing if he was lying. He put out a hand and touched Molly's arm. "We have some room to move around in now."

"It's . . . so dark. Can't see . . . anything. We can't . . . get out."

She was right about not being able to see. Fargo could have held his hand an inch from his nose, and he wouldn't have seen it at all. Molly wasn't worried about the bats anymore, though, and that was good.

"We'll get out," Fargo said. "It's no worse in here than having your eyes closed on a dark night."

"It's . . . worse."

Fargo moved closer to Molly and put his arms around her. He didn't talk. He just sat there and held her until her breathing returned to normal. It was eerie to have a woman in your arms and not be able to see her. It was almost like holding a ghost, but ghosts weren't solid, or so Fargo had heard tell.

After a while Molly's breathing slowed and then became normal again.

"If we do get out of here," Molly said, "are you sure you don't want to settle down and be a farmer? I think I can make a go of it on Tally's place."

Fargo grinned in the darkness. "I'm no farmer. And we aren't out of here yet."

"You said we'd get out. I'm almost starting to believe you."

Fargo wished he believed it himself. He said, "We'd better start moving again. Try not to skin your hands and knees too bad."

"When can we stand up?"

"Later," Fargo said. "When we get out of this tunnel."

It seemed like a long time. It seemed almost like forever. But finally they did come out of the tunnel. They practically fell out of it, in fact, which proved that Fargo had been right. They were going downward.

They found themselves in another room. Fargo stood up and breathed deeply. It was good to be out of the tunnel, though he still couldn't see anything, and he stretched to loosen his cramped limbs.

"How big is this place?" Molly asked.

Fargo said that he didn't know. He called out and tried to judge by the echo. The sound of his voice reverberated hollowly around them.

"Pretty big, I'd guess," Molly said. "What do we do now?"

"Find a way out," Fargo said. "Just like before."

"I hope it's not as small as the last way out. I don't think I could take much more of that."

"We'll have to take what we find. Unless you want to go back."

"It's a good thing I can't see you, Fargo. I'd hit you if I could."

"I'll try to stay out of your way. Let's see if we can find a way out of here."

They started working their way around the wall. The rocks were rough under Fargo's hands and irritated the cuts from the knife. He ignored the stinging pain and felt carefully, looking for fissure, a wide gap, anything.

After a while he started to wonder if there was any opening at all. Or what if it was above his head? This room of the cave was huge. It was more than a room; it was a cavern, and the ceiling was quite high. There was plenty of room on the high walls above him for an exit that he could easily miss. He told himself not to worry. If they didn't find anything, they could always go back the way they'd come. It would be difficult, but they knew it could be done. If they could locate the tunnel again.

Fargo was tired, and he was thirsty. The throbbing in his head had settled down to a steady ache, which was some improvement, but not much. He remembered a time when he'd been trapped underground in a mine in Virginia City. He'd gotten out of there, and he'd get out of the cave. No matter how bad things seemed, there was always a way.

He was still telling himself that when he heard a surprised scream from Molly.

The scream lasted for only a couple of seconds, and then it was abruptly cut off by the sound of a body hitting the ground.

Fargo didn't move. He didn't know exactly what had happened, but he guessed that Molly had somehow fallen. She hadn't fallen far, but Fargo had no way of knowing how badly she might have been hurt.

"Molly," he said. "Can you hear me?"

There was no answer, and Fargo started moving back the way he had come, careful to keep a hand on the wall all the time. He moved faster than he should have, and he stumbled a couple of times, once almost falling himself. It wouldn't do to have both of them unconscious, so he slowed down and tried to be more careful.

When he came to the tunnel they had entered from, he slowed down even more. He didn't want to fall into the same hole that Molly had. He went on for a couple of yards and then stopped. The silence in the cavern was almost overwhelming. It seemed to close in around him and press on him like the darkness.

He called Molly's name again. This time she answered.

"I'm all right, Fargo. Just had the wind knocked out of me."

"Where are you?"

"How the hell should I know? I was moving along, and all of a sudden there wasn't anything under my feet. So I fell and landed wherever it is that I am. The ground is different here, I can tell you that much. It's sandy."

That explained why she hadn't been hurt any worse than she had. Fargo said, "I'm going to see if I can get to you. Wait for me."

"Just where is it you think I'd go? Off to the nearest saloon for a drink?"

Fargo ignored that and moved very slowly in her direction, putting out his foot and feeling for the floor before every step. When he came to a spot where there was nothing under his leading foot but air, he stopped. He seemed to be standing on the verge of some kind of ledge, and he took a few seconds to consider what he could do next.

"Are you still down there?" he said after he'd thought things over.

"That's right. I haven't found the saloon yet."

"Have you looked for a way back up?"

"Looked? Has that bump on your head made you loco, Fargo? I couldn't look if I wanted to. No, that's not right. I can look all I want to, but I can't see a damn thing. Not unless you want to light a lantern for me."

Molly was getting a little touchy, not that Fargo blamed her.

"I meant had you tried to *feel* for a way back up."

"Yeah, I tried that. But there's no handhold that I can find. The wall is too slick. You can either come down here or go back to Murray. Or keep looking for a way out."

Fargo thought it over. He wasn't going back to Murray, and he wasn't going to leave Molly alone down there below, so it wasn't as if he really had a choice.

"I'm coming down," he said. "Move away from the wall."

"You be careful. I don't want you breaking a leg. I'm big, but not big enough to carry you out of this place."

Fargo planned to be careful. He sat down and scooted forward until his legs were dangling over the ledge.

"How far down is it?" he asked.

"I'd tell you if I knew," Molly said. "Not far, I guess, or I'd be a lot more addled than I am."

"Here I come, then."

Fargo pushed himself to the lip of the ledge and went sliding over. He'd done a lot of scary things in his time, but launching himself into pitch-black dark to fall who knew how far had to be one of the worst.

His feet hit the ground before he expected them to and sent a jolt all the way up his body. It nearly blew the top of his head off, but he didn't have time to think about that as he tumbled forward. He stuck out his hands to catch himself and somersaulted onto his back. When he landed, he put both hands on top of his head as if to hold it on. Then he lay still for a couple of seconds.

"You all right, Fargo?" Molly asked.

"I'd say that depends on what you mean by 'all right.' I'm alive, anyway."

"You might be better off dead. This is a hell of a place."

110

Fargo recalled his earlier notion about being in hell. "It's not hot enough," he said. "And if we were in hell, there'd at least be some light."

"Fine. This place is worse than hell, then. Are you going to get us out of it or not? I'd just as soon not spend any more time here than we have to."

Fargo sat up. His head didn't hurt any more than it had before. It didn't hurt any less, either.

He took his hands off his head and touched the ground. Molly had been right. It was more like coarse sand than rock, quite different from the floor of the cavern above them. He stood up. It took him a second or two to get his balance, and even then he felt a little bit unsteady.

"Does the ground slope?" he asked. "Or is it just me?"

"It slopes, all right," Molly said. "I don't know what that means, though. We'd better be more careful from here on out. The next fall might be a long one. There are a lot of caves down south of here, and some of them are supposed to have bottomless holes in them."

"People say that about caves," Fargo told her. "I don't much believe it. How could there be a hole without a bottom?"

"Maybe there's not, but I don't want to be the one to find out if those stories are right or wrong."

"We'll be careful," Fargo said.

He tried to decide whether to follow the wall or the slope of the ground. While he was thinking, he sniffed the air.

"Do you smell that?" he asked.

"I don't smell anything. Is there a skunk in here? We aren't around those bats, are we?"

"There aren't any bats here. I smell water. Where are you?"

"Right over here. And I don't smell any water."

"Stay right where you are and keep talking. I'm coming over to you."

Molly kept talking, mostly about bats, while Fargo made his way over to her. He took her hand and said, "Now, let's go down this little slope. Slowly."

"I hope you don't think I'm about to make any fast moves. I might be big, but I'm not crazy."

"Nobody think you're crazy. Come on."

Fargo tugged at her hand and shuffled his boots across

the grainy floor, moving carefully down the slope, which went on for yard after yard. Finally Fargo stopped.

"Can you hear that?" he asked.

The slightest of noises broke the silence that hovered all around them. It was the trickle of water.

"You were right, Fargo," Molly said. "There's water here."

"And I can use some of it."

He pulled her hand again, and they went on toward the sound. After a few steps, Fargo's boots sloshed in water. Fargo let go of Molly's hand and knelt down, feeling around him. There was a shallow rivulet not more than two or three inches deep running through the sand. Cold water stung the cuts on his hands.

"There must be a spring down here," he said, scooping water up into his hands.

"I can't see what you're doing, Fargo," Molly said. "Are you going to drink any of that water? It might be poison."

"And it might not. I don't see how it could be, and I'm too thirsty not to give it a try. If I die, you can pass it up."

"To hell with that. I'm as thirsty as you are."

Fargo felt Molly kneel down beside him as he brought the water to his lips. It was cold and tasted as sweet as any water he'd ever drunk.

When he'd drunk his fill, he said, "Now, let's get out of here."

"How are we going to get out?" Molly said. "I don't see any doors opening anywhere around here."

"This water has to go somewhere," Fargo told her. "We'll follow it."

"What if it just goes into a hole in the ground? What if it flows into some big underground lake? What if it just disappears under a wall?"

Fargo knew that any of those things was possible. But he said, "I think it must go out of here. Maybe it even goes to the river."

"It's just a trickle. I'm not even sure you can tell which way it's moving."

Fargo put his hand in the water and waited. It flowed slowly but definitely to his right.

"I can tell," he said. He took Molly's hand and stood up, bringing her along with him. "We're going this way."

It wasn't easy to walk in a straight line in the total darkness. In fact, it would have been impossible if Fargo hadn't kept right to the edge of the water, splashing his boot in it to be sure he didn't stray.

They walked for a while and then had another drink and rested. Fargo could tell that Molly was tiring, but he was determined not to rest for long. He got back to his feet. He wanted to get out of the cave, if that was possible, and the sooner, the better. He gave Molly a tug, and they started walking again.

After they had been moving along for quite a while, Molly said, "Now I smell something. It stinks."

Fargo smelled it, too, and he knew what it had to be.

"Bat shit," he said.

"Bats? Oh, my sweet Jesus."

"You should be glad we're getting close to them," Fargo said.

"They'll get all over us. They'll tangle in my hair. Why should I be glad?"

"Because the bats will have a way to get outside. If they can get out, we can get out."

Molly thought that over for a minute. "I never thought I'd be glad to smell bat shit, but I guess I am."

And then they walked head-on into a wall of rock.

15

They weren't walking fast, so they weren't hurt, though Fargo's nose was a little flatter than it had been.

"That's it," Molly said when she'd recovered from the unexpected jolt. "The end of the line. We aren't getting out of here, Fargo."

"The water goes out, and we can smell the bats. We're getting out."

Fargo let go of Molly's hand and bent down to kneel on the sand. There was a small opening at the base of the wall, though not large enough to slither through.

"The bats must be in another cave that's connected to this one by this hole where the water goes out," Fargo said. "They like a cave with water in it, and a high ceiling to catch the warm air. There must be another opening somewhere in this wall leading to the other cave. If there weren't, the smell wouldn't be so strong."

"Look up," Molly said, touching his shoulder. "Is that light up there?"

Fargo looked up. Thirty or forty feet above them there was a thin line of light, unless he was imagining it.

"We'd never be able to climb up there," Molly said. "Not in the dark. Maybe not even if we could see."

"If we can't go over, we have to go under," Fargo said.

He started scooping sand away from the bottom of the wall. Molly heard what he was doing and got down on her knees to help. Before long they had made an opening big enough to slide through. A faint light shone under the wall.

"You first," Fargo said.

Molly didn't wait for him to say it again. She flopped

down on her belly and wormed beneath the wall. Fargo was right behind her, her feet practically in his face. When he stood up on the other side and brushed off the sand, he found himself in another cavern. He could almost make out the contours of this one because across from them there was a slit in the cave wall, no wider than three feet across. Light shone outside it, and looking at it hurt Fargo's eyes.

Above them the bats stirred. It was as if a giant sigh had gone around the cavern. The smell of their droppings was almost overwhelming.

"Let's get out of this smell," Molly said. "I don't want to be here when they wake up."

"They won't start flying out of here until dusk," Fargo told her.

"I don't care. I want out of here now."

Molly started off across the floor of the cave and had gone eight or nine steps before her feet slipped out from under her on the slick guano. She landed on her rear and sat there until Fargo made his way to her.

"You have to be careful when you're walking in shit," he said.

"I appreciate the good advice. Now help me up from here."

Fargo did as he was asked, and Molly stood up, holding onto his hand to steady herself. Clinging together, they went toward the light.

When they reached it, Molly shoved through, with Fargo right behind her. The rivulet ran out of the cave into a small pool that overflowed on down the side of the hill that they found themselves standing on. It was late afternoon, and there were clouds in the sky, but the hazy sun was almost blinding to them because they had been in the cave for more than twelve hours. They fell down on the grass and closed their eyes.

After a while Molly sat up and said, "I'm filthy. I've been crawling around in a cave all day, and I have bat shit all over me. I'm going into that pool."

"With your clothes on?" Fargo asked.

"No. I plan to take them off and wash them out after I've bathed. I'll trust you to be a gentleman and keep your eyes off me."

"I'm glad you trust me that much," Fargo said.

Molly started to take off her shirt, but she stopped and said, "You're not being a gentleman."

"That's one thing I've never been accused of. Do you mind?"

Molly grinned and said that she didn't. "But maybe I shouldn't bathe. Murray must know we're gone by now. You don't think he'll find us here, do you?"

Fargo didn't see how it was possible. Murray probably didn't even know about the connecting caves. He'd surely checked on his prisoners by now and discovered they were gone, but he probably thought they were just wandering around in the depths of the cave or trapped in the tunnel. Or maybe he was smarter than that. Maybe he'd search for them.

"I think we can take a quick bath, and then we'd better get ourselves out of sight."

"What do you mean 'we' can take a bath?"

"I think you know what I mean."

Molly grinned again. "All right, then, come on."

Molly stripped off her clothing and waded into the pool. Fargo removed his buckskins but paused long enough to admire the action of Molly's ample but firm backside as she moved away from him into the water. It was the kind of sight he never got tired of. When she entered the water, she turned to face him, and Fargo went in after her.

The pool was only a couple of feet deep and the water was cold, but it felt good on Fargo's skin as it washed off the grime and sludge. He ducked his head under the surface and came sputtering to the top, flinging his hair back out of his eyes. The pain in his head was easing, and the cuts on his hands no longer stung.

Molly was sitting nearby, watching him. She raised herself to float closer, and when she got beside him, she reached under the water and grasped a part of him that was standing at attention.

"I thought you might be in that condition," she said. "Even after all that just happened to us, you're still as stiff as a fence post."

Fargo nodded and said, "It's your fault. Looking at you got me that way."

"Then I guess I'll have to do something about it," Molly said.

She turned to straddle him and sat on his rod, letting it slide right into her. Even in the water she was slick and ready for him. When she had settled herself on him, her large breasts flattened against his chest, the nipples poking into him like small hot stones.

"You have a lot of scars," she said, putting her finger on one. "Where'd you get that?"

"I picked it up from a grizzly."

"Does he have a scar, too?"

"Nope," Fargo said. "He's dead."

"I'm not surprised," Molly said, giving a little wiggle. "How are we going to do this?"

"I figure we'll find a way," Fargo said.

"I bet you're right," Molly said, and she pressed the palms of her hands on the tops of his shoulders, raising and lowering herself on him. Her body was buoyant in the water, and a couple of times she almost bounced too high, but Fargo held onto her hips so that she didn't slip away.

It wasn't long before she was churning the water into a froth. Her head fell back, and she opened her mouth. Fargo knew what was about to happen, but he couldn't do a thing to stop it. He was about at his own limit, and when she started yelling, he shot into her, bucking up off the bottom of the pool with each volley.

"YeeeeeHaaaaaaw! YeeeeeHaaaaaw!" Molly cried, kicking out with her legs on either side of Fargo and sending little waves to the shore.

When she was finished, she collapsed against him, and they sat quietly for a minute or so.

"I hope Murray didn't hear that," Molly said.

Fargo hoped so, too. He figured Molly had frightened the wildlife for a couple of miles around.

"We'd better clean up and get out of here," he said, and they did, washing out their clothes and putting them on wet. It was uncomfortable, but Fargo didn't think it would be smart to hang around there much longer.

By the time they were dressed, it was dusk, and the bats started to come out of the cave. At first there were only a few of them, but within a couple of minutes there were so many that they formed a black cloud overhead. The humming of their wings filled the air as they flew away, shadowed against the darkening sky and showing no interest at all in Fargo and Molly.

"I told you they wouldn't tangle in your hair," Fargo said.

"That doesn't mean I have to like them." Molly shuddered. "Let's get out of here."

They started walking. Fargo looked back after they were well away from the pool, and bats were still flying out of the cave. There had been thousands of them in there, he thought.

Molly didn't look back. She wanted to know where they were going.

"To get us some horses. Judging from what you told me, I figure it's too far back to the farms to walk."

"Yes, but I don't know where we're getting any horses."

"From Murray. He might even have my horse there. I'd like to have him back."

"How can you find the entrance to the cave we were in?"

"I can find it. You might say being able to do things like that is the business I'm in."

"What business is that?"

Fargo explained a little bit about what being a Trailsman meant and how he'd spent most of his life guiding people from one place to another, finding trails others couldn't, and getting out of places most people didn't even go.

"Like that cave," Molly said.

"Not like that. I'd just as soon never have to do anything like that again."

"You sure have an instinct for it. I never thought we'd get out of there, but I'm glad I trusted you."

Fargo didn't say that there was an element of luck involved. If she wanted to believe he could find a trail even in darkness so black that you couldn't see, then let her. Besides, he thought, there might even be some truth in it.

He had a lot less trouble finding the horses than he'd had finding a way out of the caverns, and it didn't take as long. The horses were hobbled in a little grove of trees not far from the entrance to the cave where Murray and his men were hiding out. Among them was Fargo's Ovaro.

Fargo and Molly crouched on top of the hill, and the

cave was below them. Night had fallen, but the moon was coming up, making the landscape seem almost to be shining in bright daylight compared to the darkness of the cave. There was the glow of a fire from inside Murray's hideout.

"Does he have a guard on the horses?" Molly whispered.

Fargo didn't see anybody, but that didn't mean there was no one there.

"Maybe so, maybe not. We'll sit here awhile and watch."

They made themselves as comfortable as they could and waited. The night was cool, and a breeze rippled the grass. There was no movement in the trees other than the horses and the leaves rustling on the trees. But Fargo waited awhile longer.

His caution paid off when a shadow finally separated itself from one of the trees and stood aside to urinate. Fargo could hear the splashing as the stream hit the tree trunk.

"He'll move away from there," Molly said.

"And when he does, I'll get him," Fargo said, slipping the knife out of his boot. "Wait here."

He went silently down the hill and into the trees. The guard was just finishing his business, shaking off the last few drops, when Fargo came up behind him and put a forearm across his throat.

The man tried to cry out, but Fargo clamped down on him and then hit him in the temple with the hilt of the knife. The man went limp, and Fargo lowered him to the ground. He located the Ovaro and led it back up the hill.

"Can you ride bareback?" he asked Molly.

"What do you think?"

Fargo didn't answer. He took hold of the Ovaro's mane and swung himself up on its back. Then he reached a hand to Molly and pulled her up behind him.

"How long do you think it will take before Murray figures out we've gotten away?" she asked.

"He'll know when his guard wakes up. That might be an hour or two. We'll be long gone by then."

"Well, by God, I'm glad to hear it," Molly said.

16

Lem and Abby were happy and surprised to see Fargo and Molly again. Fargo told what had happened to them, leaving out the part about the bath.

Abby cooked some bacon and beans, and while Molly and Fargo ate, Lem filled them in on what had happened in their absence.

"We thought sure they'd killed the two of you," Lem said. "They sure as hell killed Alf."

"What about his house?" Fargo asked.

"It's still standing. I figured they'd burn it, but you and Molly must've scared them off. When we found Molly's horse, we went on over to Talley's place, but it was still standing, too. Looks like Molly's house and barn were the only places they burned. Murray must not like her a whole lot."

"Could be that there's another reason," Fargo said.

"If there's another reason, I'd like to know what it is," Molly said.

Fargo chewed some beans and then said, "I haven't quite got it all figured out yet. I had a lot of time to think while we were wandering around in the dark, and I have a few ideas. I talked to Angel, too, and she said something I didn't quite understand."

"When did you talk to her?" Abby asked, suspicion edging her voice. "She's been gone a while now."

Fargo didn't think it would be wise to explain the circumstances under which he'd last talked to Angel, at least not to Abby. Judging by the grin on Molly's face, Molly already had a pretty good idea.

"You'll remember I spent some time watching Angel

while she was staying here," Fargo said. "She told me some things."

"What things?" Lem said.

Fargo told them about the death of Murray's wife and how Murray had come to blame the farmers instead of the people who'd actually done the killing.

"That's just plain crazy," Lem said. "But then we already knew Murray was crazy for revenge. You haven't told us anything new, except one more of his reasons for going after us."

"That's not the whole story. Angel said that there was more to it."

"Well?" Abby said. "Tell us what it was."

"That's just it. Angel wouldn't tell me. She said she wasn't even sure herself. Paul was the one their father trusted, probably because he wasn't a woman."

"A woman can keep a secret," Molly said. "And a woman can be just as good in a fight as any man, especially the men around here. I didn't see any of *them* coming to help Alf Wesley."

"I wanted to," Lem told her. "Fargo made me stay in case they came around here."

"No offense," Molly said. "I didn't mean you, in particular. But the whole bunch of them is too scared to go after Murray."

"Now that we know where he's hiding out, we can change their minds," Lem said. "First thing in the morning, I'll ride around to all the neighbors and call a meeting. We can go after Murray in his hideout and finish him off."

Fargo shoved back his plate. The beans and bacon had filled him, and Abby had boiled some coffee that was strong and hot, steaming in a thick mug. Fargo drank some of the coffee before he spoke.

"I wouldn't count on him being there," he said. "He's not going to stay around, knowing that Molly and I got loose. He'll have found himself another place by morning."

"You're right, I guess," Lem said. "I wasn't thinking straight."

"You couldn't have got that bunch of lollygaggers to go with you, anyway," Molly said. "You and me and Fargo would have been about all."

"I would have gone," Abby said. "I can shoot as well as you can."

Molly gave her a measuring look.

"I might not be as big as you, but I'm just as mean," Abby told her.

Molly laughed. "You just might be, at that. But just the four of us wouldn't stand a chance, even if we could flush Murray out of wherever it is he's hiding now. We have to think of something better than that."

"Maybe in the morning," Lem said. "It's mighty late for thinking."

"Too late for you to go back to Talley's place, too," Fargo told Molly. "It wouldn't do for you to be riding out alone, not with Murray still on the loose."

"She can stay in the spare room," Abby said, "and you . . ."

"Can stay in the barn," Fargo said. "I knew that already."

He didn't really mind staying in the barn. In fact, he thought it was a good idea. You never knew, with two women like Molly and Abby in the house, what one of them might take it into her head to do. And if both of them had the same notion and showed up in his room, Fargo might find himself in a heap of trouble. Or some other kind of heap that would be more interesting, but maybe even more complicated. It was the kind of situation he preferred to avoid, so he went out to the barn without complaint. He spread his blanket on the hay and lay down, realizing only then how tired he was. He was asleep within seconds.

Angel woke him just before sunup. The light in the barn was dim at best, but Fargo could see well enough to tell who was crouching near his foot, shaking it lightly, as soon as he opened his eyes. He sat up and rubbed his eyes, thinking that he hadn't had nearly enough sleep.

"Don't you think it's a little bit dangerous for you to be here?" he asked.

Angel sat on the floor, her knees drawn up and her arms clasped around her legs. She looked at Fargo over the tops of her knees and said, "I know it's dangerous, all right, but I came to do you a favor. Do you want to listen?"

Fargo yawned and sat up. "I'm listening."

"I didn't think you'd get away in that cave. I still don't know how you did it, but you made Pa really mad."

"As I remember it, he's never been a very happy man, anyhow," Fargo said. "So I guess he hasn't changed all that much."

"No, he hasn't. But this time he's worse than he usually is. He's sorry he didn't kill you when he had the chance, and he blames me for that."

"Seems like I ought to thank you."

"You should. It was a weakness in me, and I know it, just like coming here now is a weakness. Pa doesn't like weakness in a man, or in a woman, either."

"I wouldn't call it a weakness," Fargo said. "And I do thank you."

"You're welcome, then. But we've talked about it enough. What you'd better do is get yourself out of here, because Pa and the gang aren't far behind me. He's coming to get you, and anybody else that's here, no matter what. He'd skin me alive if he knew I came to warn you."

"Won't he find out?"

"I don't care if he does. I'm not going to stay around any longer. He never really cared for me, not the way he did for Paul. He thinks a woman is prone to weakness, and I guess I've proved him right about that."

"Maybe you just don't enjoy killing as much as he does."

"He doesn't enjoy it. It's just something he has to do." Angel unclasped her hands and stood up. "I have to go now. You'd better get yourself ready. He'll be here mighty quick."

She didn't say anything more, just turned and went down the ladder. By the time Fargo got his boots on, she was gone.

There was no time to plan anything elaborate. Lem wanted to send Abby to fetch help from the nearest farm, which happened to be Frank Conner's.

"The only one there will be Frank," Abby said. "And maybe one hired hand. You'd be just as well off if I stayed here. I can shoot as well as Frank, and better than any hired hand he might have. You just want to get me out of the way."

She'd seen through Lem's plan, and he gave in reluctantly.

"You can stay, then," he said. "What're we gonna do, Fargo?"

"Try to catch Murray's bunch in a crossfire. Molly and I will set up in the barn, and you and Abby can get ready in the house. We might kill enough of them so that they won't stay around long. If Angel was telling the truth, they won't know we're waiting for them."

"I'd still like to know how you and Angel got so close," Abby said. "Thicker than thieves. I find it hard to believe she'd come to warn you and betray her father."

"Don't worry about that," Molly said, helping Fargo out. "Worry about staying alive for the next hour or so."

Abby looked at Molly thoughtfully, then nodded. Fargo and Molly went to the barn.

"Looks like you get around even more than I thought, Fargo," Molly said. "I never would have thought Abby would give in to you."

Fargo didn't tell her that he was the one who'd done the giving in. He said, "I can be mighty persuasive when I try. Do you want the loft or the doors here?"

"It's not easy shooting down at an angle, but I can do it. I'll take the loft."

While she climbed the ladder, Fargo dragged a couple of wooden boxes over to the door of the barn and stacked them so that he could use them for cover. It wasn't much cover, and he didn't have much of a plan, but it was the best he could come up with. Now there was nothing to do but wait for Murray to show up.

Time dragged along with no sign of the gang. It was well past sunup, and there was no sign of anyone.

"What do you think, Fargo?" Molly called from the loft. "Did Angel lie to you?"

"I don't know why she would. And it sure sounded like she was telling me the truth."

"Maybe they'll show up, then," Molly said, but there was no conviction in her voice.

Another few minutes passed, and then Fargo heard shooting. It wasn't coming from anywhere nearby, but Fargo thought he could guess the location.

"Connor's farm," he said.

"That's right," Molly said. "Angel lied to you. What do we do now?"

"We go help Conner," Fargo said.

                    *   *   *

By the time Fargo arrived at the farm, there wasn't much he could do for Conner, who was already beyond help. He'd been shot, and then someone had dragged him outside his house and tied him upright to the scarecrow in his vegetable garden. His head drooped down on his chest, and his body slumped against the ropes that held him.

There was nothing Fargo could do for Angel, either. She was tied up hand and foot and propped against the side of Connor's house. Unlike Conner, however, she was still alive.

Murray and his men were waiting when Fargo rode up. Murray sat up straight on his horse like a general in command of an army. His beard stirred in the breeze, and he looked at Fargo with his mad eyes. His men were lined up on either side of him. They had their pistols and rifles pointed straight at Fargo.

"My daughter betrayed me," Murray said. His voice was deep and strong. "There are traitors in every army, but I never thought there would be one in my own family."

"He caught me," Angel said, her voice shaky. "He made me tell him. He's going to kill me."

Fargo didn't have any reason to doubt her. Murray was crazy enough to kill anybody, even his daughter.

"He's not going to kill you," Fargo said.

"That's where you're wrong," Murray told him. "I'm in command here, not you, Mr. Fargo, and she will die by my orders. And you will follow her to hell."

"Not if you get there first," Fargo said, drawing his pistol.

Murray stared in blank surprise. He clearly hadn't expected Fargo to do anything so foolhardy, not with twelve or fifteen guns on him.

But then Murray didn't know that Fargo wasn't alone. Lem, Abby, and Molly had circled around behind the gang, and now they came riding through the cornfield, firing as they came.

Two of Murray's men pitched off their rearing horses as the others turned to meet the unforeseen threat.

Fargo fired at Murray, but the big man reacted quickly, spurring his horse and making a run for Connor's house. As he rode, he fired two shots at Angel. At least one of them struck her, and she fell sideways to the ground. Then Murray was around the house and gone.

Fargo would have pursued him, but he had to deal with the remaining gang members, some of whom had turned their attention back to him. For a few minutes the shooting was loud and fast, and then it was over, smoke drifting in the air and the smell of gunpowder filling Fargo's nostrils.

Four of the gang members were dead, and the rest were hightailing it. Nobody went after them, as Fargo was sure it wouldn't do any good. And he wanted to see if there was anything that could be done about Angel.

Abby got to her first and lifted her to a sitting position. There was blood on the front of Angel's shirt, but she was alive and her eyes were open.

Abby tore the shirt off and Fargo got a look at the wound as he came up. He didn't think it was serious. The only bad thing about it was its location.

"He shot her in the same shoulder you did," Abby said. "The son of a bitch."

Lem shook his head in disapproval of his daughter's language.

"You ought not to talk any such way," he said, "but a man that would shoot his own child is a son of a bitch in my book, too."

"We'll take you back to our place," Abby said. "We'll take care of you again. You won't have to deal with that son of a . . ."

"Hold it," Lem said. "We can take care of her without saying what her daddy is. Fargo, you go cut down Frank. Him hanging there like that's just not right."

Fargo and Molly went to the scarecrow. Fargo took his knife out of his boot and cut the ropes that held Conner up. Molly caught him as he sagged forward and lowered him to the ground.

"Those bastards," she said. "But we got four of them. I say let the buzzards have them."

"We need to do a little better than that for them," Fargo said. "But not much. Can you round up some help?"

"There's not that many of us left. And if this keeps on, there won't be any."

"It won't keep on," Fargo said.

"What are you going to do to stop it."

Fargo shook his head and told her he didn't know.

17

The next few days passed without any more incursions by Murray. Fargo figured he was looking for a new hideout, since Angel had told them where he'd stayed after leaving the cave. The drunken doctor had come out and removed the bullet from Angel's shoulder, and she was healing again. Fargo and Lem tried to decide what to do about Murray.

"There aren't that many places around here he could go," Lem said. "If we could find out where he is, we'd go after him."

"Who's *we*," Fargo wanted to know.

"I've talked to Cass Ellis and Bob Tabor. Both of them would throw in with us. And they think they could find some others. Murray shouldn't have hung Frank from that scarecrow. That made people madder than anything he's done so far."

"What about Rip Johnson?" Fargo asked.

Rip had been by a couple of times already, trying to get Abby's attention, hoping to make some time with her.

"Rip's ready to ride anytime we say. He told me to let him know first thing, just as soon as we decide on a plan, so he could be ready. He and Frank were friends, just like he and Tom were. He's lucky he wasn't killed like them, and he knows it."

Fargo thought about that and decided to ride over to Talley's place, or Molly's, since it was hers now by virtue of the bank and her own persistence.

He stopped in Angel's room first. She was propped up on some pillows and smiled when he came in.

"I guess we're even now, Fargo. I stuck up for you when

Pa wanted to kill you, and you stuck up for me the other day. I was just about sure Pa was going to kill me."

"He almost did. I need to know where he's hiding out these days."

Fargo had already asked that question more than once, and Angel kept putting him off. He wasn't sure if she really didn't know anything or if she was still protecting her father even though he'd shot her.

"I'd tell you if I knew. He could be back in the cave, though. That's like something he'd do. He'd try to outsmart you, and if he believed you wouldn't expect him to be there, he might head straight for it. It would be worth a try."

Fargo had already considered that possibility. He didn't think Murray would go back to the cave. It was too easy to get trapped in a cave if you didn't know the way out, and Fargo didn't think Murray would want to exit by the route Fargo had used. It was too uncomfortable, and it took too long. And Fargo would know where he'd be coming out.

"We could check the cave," Fargo said, not really meaning it. "There's something else that's been bothering me."

Angel tried to sit up a little straighter, hardly wincing at the pain she must have felt.

"What's bothering you?" she asked.

There were a lot of things. Fargo had a whole list of them, but he didn't want to go through them with Angel. So he told her one of them.

"Seems to me your father always knows what's going on with the farmers. He knows when the funerals are, and he knows who's going to be there. He knows whose house the bodies will be in, and he knows who'll be sitting up with them. I don't see how he does it."

"I don't know, either, but I see what you mean. If Paul were alive, he could tell you. Pa always let him in on the plans. He never told me anything. He let me ride with him, but that was only because I wouldn't stay behind. You know something, Fargo?"

Fargo didn't like guessing games, so he didn't reply. Angel apparently didn't expect him to, and she answered her own question.

"I should have left Pa long ago. I must have been crazy to stay with him when I saw what he was doing."

"I'm not too clear on what he's doing." Fargo said. "You told me a while back that there was more to it than I knew, but you never explained what you meant by it."

"That's because I don't know much more than you do. But Pa and Paul used to go off all the time to discuss their plans. That's probably when they met with their spy."

"How do you know there was a spy?"

"You said it yourself. Pa always knew everything. There had to be a spy. I thought you knew that. I just can't tell you who it was because I was never there when they met."

Fargo had figured out the spy part for himself. He even thought he knew who the spy was, which was why he was going to see Molly.

"You must have some idea about the plans," he said.

He had a vague idea, himself, but he couldn't quite make sense of all the ideas rattling around in his head.

"All I know is that Pa was upset with everybody when Ma was killed," Angel said. "He hates the farmers, he hates the free-staters, he hates the slaveholders. Sometimes that's all he can talk about. I don't know how he thinks he can whip all of them, but for some reason he started with the farmers."

Fargo knew why Murray had started with the farmers. It was the smart thing to do because he could whip them more easily than the other groups. If he had mixed it up with the others, the army would have gotten involved, and that would have been the end of things for Murray right there. Which was why Fargo couldn't figure out how Murray could go beyond the farmers.

"He talks about the South a lot, too," Angel said. "Sometimes I thought he might want to go there to live. But he doesn't. He says that nobody can run him off and that he's staying right here where he belongs."

That was a new fact for Fargo to think about. He wasn't sure that it meant anything, but maybe it fit somewhere with all the other things he was mulling over. He thought that he might be able to pull it all together when he talked to Molly.

"Where will you go?" Fargo asked Angel.

"I've been thinking about that. I'd like to stay here if the people would have me. I'm willing to work, and I can learn about farming. They might not want me, though. I've been fighting against them for a good while. I wouldn't blame them if they hated me."

"You should talk to Abby about it."

"I don't know what to say to her. It's my fault that Jed was killed, and they were going to be married."

"You said Jed got what he deserved."

"I don't feel that way now. He was right all along. If I'd listened to him, he'd be alive, but I thought I had to stick by my family. You can see where that got me."

There wasn't much Fargo could say to that. He said, "You might be surprised at how forgiving people can be if they know you're sorry for what you did. I don't think Abby will blame you for anything after she hears what you have to say. She'll help you find a place around here."

"That would be nice, but I don't know if I can ask her. It's not right, what I've done."

"People change," Fargo said, though in his experience the ones who did were few and far between. "You talk to Abby. You might find out she's changed a little, too."

Angel said she'd try, and Fargo left to pay his visit to Molly.

Molly was feeding the chickens when Fargo got there, sticking her hand into a bag of corn and flinging it out in wide swaths. As soon as the grain hit the ground, the chickens would snap it up. Or they'd snap something up. Since they were in the chicken yard, the chickens would sometimes miss the corn and peck at their own droppings. After watching them for a few seconds, Fargo thought it might be a while before he wanted to eat fried chicken again.

"Hey, Fargo," Molly said when she saw him standing there. "Did you come by to help me feed the chickens?" She gave him a wicked grin. "Or did you have something else in mind?"

"I had something else in mind," Fargo said, "but it might not be what you're thinking."

"That's too bad, but it's nice to see you anyway. I have to put this corn in the barn. Come on along."

Molly went off toward the barn, and Fargo followed behind. She put the bag of corn in a barrel so nothing would get into it. She covered the barrel, dusted off her hands, and turned to Fargo.

"All right. If this isn't about what I was hoping it was, what is it about?"

"We need to have a little talk," Fargo said.

"We're talking already. You have a particular subject in mind?"

"Peter Murray."

"That's one thing I'd just as soon not talk about. He's not a very pleasant subject."

Fargo thought it might get less pleasant before their conversation was over. He said, "Do you want to talk here in the barn or go inside?"

"It's nice enough here in the barn." Molly sat on the covered barrel. "Find yourself a seat and let's talk."

Fargo pulled a nail keg over and sat down on it. He was at a lower level than Molly, and she had to look down at him to see his face.

"Now, what is it about Murray that you want to tell me?" Molly asked.

Fargo told her what Angel had said about the death of Murray's wife and the way Murray felt because of it. Then he talked about how Murray always knew what was going to happen and where everyone was going to be.

"We've talked about that last part before. At Jed's funeral. Remember?"

Fargo said that he did. "I've been thinking about it some more. If Murray knew everything that was going on, somebody had to tell him."

"I figured that, but I don't know who it could be. There are a lot of people around here, and I can't keep watch on all of them."

Fargo didn't really think she'd tried to keep watch. He said, "Only a few people knew where Paul Murray was buried. And of the ones who knew, three of them are dead."

Molly looked at him through hooded eyes.

"What are you trying to say, Fargo? That I have something to do with what Murray finds out about things?"

"It could be that way," Fargo told her.

"But you don't think so, do you. You know me better than that, Fargo."

Fargo wasn't sure you could ever know people well enough to predict what they might or might not do, no matter how long you'd known them.

"I'm not sure what to think," he said. "Your house and barn were burned, but not any of the others. I asked myself about why that might be."

"It could be that Murray hates me more than the others. And that means I'm not the one passing information to him."

"Or it could be that he just wanted people to think he hates you. You have another house and barn already, and it didn't take you long to get them."

"I don't like the way this is going, Fargo. You might want to think it over before you say anything else."

"I've already thought about it. I don't have much else to say."

"That's good, because I'm about through listening. Get on with it."

"It's about Jed," Fargo said. "I don't think anybody in the Murray gang killed him."

"I don't know what makes you say that. Everybody knows he was killed in the fight at Lem's barn."

"He was killed in the fight, all right, but it wasn't the Murrays who killed him. I've been pretty sure of that all along. They were on horseback, but the way the bullet went in Jed's head showed that whoever shot him was standing behind him. Murray wanted him dead, all right, but he had to be sure the job was done. The one way to do that would be to have somebody there who could take care of it. It would have been easy for somebody who was already at the party to come up behind and kill Jed in all the confusion."

"Why would someone besides the Murrays want to kill Jed?"

"Because they wanted to get rid of him. Maybe whoever did it was jealous."

Molly slid off the barrel and stood facing Fargo.

"Are you saying that I killed him because I was jealous of Abby? And that I was spying on everybody for the same reason?"

"It makes sense," Fargo said. "You knew where Paul was buried, and that's important. Not just the general area. Everybody knew that. But Murray went right to the grave and dug in the right place. I was there and saw it. Somebody had to tell him just exactly where the grave was."

Molly drew herself up a little straighter. She towered over Fargo, who continued sitting on the nail keg.

"You're going to make me mad in a minute if you keep on like this," Molly said.

"You can settle down," Fargo told her. "I don't really think it was you. It could have been, though, and I wanted to make sure it wasn't."

"And you're sure now?"

"I'm sure. You wouldn't be so mad at me if you were guilty."

Molly relaxed. She grinned and sat back down on the barrel.

"How do you know I'm not lying to you?"

"You could be, but I don't think so. There's somebody else who fits all the facts even better than you do."

Molly thought a second and said, "Rip Johnson."

"That's right. Rip. I asked Lem if Rip would be willing to fight with the rest of us, and he said that Rip was ready to go, and that he wanted to know as soon as anything was decided. I figure he wants to know first so he can get word to Murray. And when you think about it, it was mighty convenient that his wife was the only one killed when Murray raided his place. Everybody was drunk, but Rip might not have been as drunk as he wanted us to think. He might even have pushed his wife out of the house or told her to go outside. The others were too drunk to know if he did."

Molly's mouth twisted in disgust. "And him doing all the crying about her being dead. He was probably glad to get her out of the way so he could start working on Abby."

"He's already been sniffing around. His house and barn weren't burned, either, but then only yours were."

"Don't get started on that again. If you want to know, I think Murray did that because he thought I might leave if he did. I'm the only one around here with guts enough to stand up to him now that Jed's gone, and he'd be glad to get rid of me. But I'm not all that easy to get run off."

"On the other hand, he didn't burn any of the other

houses," Fargo said. "Why not? He wanted to get rid of everybody else."

"What if he wants the houses?" Molly asked.

"What would he do with houses?"

"It's more than just houses. It's farms. Let's say he runs everybody off. The farms will still be here, and Murray and his gang can take them. Rip would be staying, since he's in with Murray, but he'd get a better farm. Lem's. And he'd get Abby into the bargain. Or that's what he thinks. Abby would never stand still for it. She'd either kill him, or he'd have to kill her."

Fargo thought over what Molly had said. He'd always thought there had to be more than just revenge in Murray's mind. Power and revenge and property. It made sense. Fargo remembered Angel's comments about Murray's feeling for the South.

"You might be right," Fargo told Molly. "Murray could have the idea that he can set up his own little state here, maybe seal it off, or even pull out of the Union. He'd have a hell of a time defending it, though."

"He wouldn't have to. The army's already got its hands full, and nobody else is going to do anything. Before long, the whole country could be at war, and nobody's going to pay any attention to what's going on in some little farm area here. Who knows? Murray might wind up running the whole territory."

Fargo thought it was barely possible. Murray had the military bearing to draw people to him, and he had the madness necessary to believe he could do anything. And he didn't care who got hurt or killed in the process, as long as he got what he wanted. Taking the land from the farmers would give him the revenge he was looking for and put him in a position to become a far more powerful figure than he already was.

"Now all we have to do is stop him," Molly said. "How are we going to do it."

"I don't quite have that figured out yet," Fargo told her.

18

"One thing we have to do," Lem said when he and Fargo talked things over that night, "is find out where Murray is. We can't do anything else until we do that."

"We'll let Rip tell us," Fargo said.

"Rip won't tell you the truth about anything. He's always been able to look a man in the eye and tell the biggest whopper you ever heard. You'll never even get him to admit what he's been doing. If he's been doing it. I still can't believe it of him."

"I could be wrong about him," Fargo said, "but I don't think so. The way I lay it out, everything points to him."

"I know that. You make a good case. But I've known Rip for five or six years, lived here beside him, and worked with him all that time. I hate to think he'd turned on his neighbors like that."

"You don't seem too interested in having him as a son-in-law, no matter how long you've known him."

"Well, that's a different story. He's a little lazy, he let his place get run down, and he's not the man for Abby. Jed was more what I had in mind. He had backbone, and he didn't mind a little hard work. I was hoping Abby could find somebody like that. Or maybe somebody like you."

"I'm not cut out for farming, as much as I admire Abby. She's a fine woman, and she deserves better than me."

"Be hard to find anybody like that around here. Be hard to find anybody at all if we don't stop Murray. But Rip's not going to help with that."

"He is," Fargo said. "He's just not going to know he's doing it."

And he told Lem what he wanted him to do.

*   *   *

Early the next morning, while the dew was still on the fields, Lem rode to Rip's house and called him outside.

"We'll be riding out to get Murray tomorrow," Lem said, sitting easy and relaxed in the saddle.

Rip stood on his little front porch and looked up at him, squinting his eyes against the bright morning sun.

"Who's going to be in the posse?" he asked.

"You will be, I hope," Lem said.

"I'll go. I've already told you that. But who else? How many?"

"Just about everybody living around here said they'd be willing to ride, but I wanted to let you know first. We can for sure count on Cass and Bob. Molly Doyle. Fargo. Me and Abby. And Angel Murray."

"Good Lord. Are you telling me she's on our side now? That she'd ride against her own daddy?"

"She probably wouldn't be doing it if he hadn't tried to kill her," Lem said. "There's something about having your pa shoot at you that has a way of changing your mind about him."

Rip nodded his agreement. "I can see that, I guess. You sure you want Abby along? It's going to be plenty dangerous if you find Murray. He's not going to give up just because you ask him to. There'll be shooting."

"Abby says she won't stay behind, danger or not. And we'll find Murray, all right. Fargo says he knows where he's hiding."

Rip frowned at the mention of Fargo's name.

"I don't think Fargo's as smart as he thinks he is. Where does he say Murray's located?"

"He's in a cave over by the big river. He had Fargo prisoner there for a while, before he got away."

"And Fargo thinks Murray's still there?"

"That's what he says. It'll take us a while to get there, and Fargo better be right about it. If he's not, we could be in big trouble. What with most of the able-bodied men riding out, all our homes will be left wide open. Murray could just sneak in and take 'em over."

Rip seemed to think about that for a second or two before saying, "Now, why would Murray want to do that?"

136

"I don't have the least idea. It was just something that worried me."

"You don't have to worry about it." Rip's voice was confident. "We'll catch him in that cave and bottle him up. That'll be the end of him."

"That's what I'm hoping," Lem said.

"Did he take the bait?" Fargo asked.

"You bet," Lem said. "Like the biggest catfish in the Missouri. Swallowed it hook, line, sinker and all. You sure you can follow him?"

"I can follow anybody."

Lem looked skeptical. "He might spot you."

Fargo grinned. "He'll never know I'm within fifty miles of him."

Angel had known he was following her, he thought. Or she'd guessed he was. But she was expecting him to follow her. Rip didn't know anybody was onto him, and he was probably confident that they hadn't figured out about him and Murray yet.

"I hope you're right," Lem said. "If he catches you, we'll never find out where Murray's hiding."

"You don't have a thing to worry about," Fargo said. "I'll find out, and then we'll get him."

Lem shook his head doubtfully. "I sure hope you're right about that."

Fargo hoped so, too.

There had been a little rain the day before, not much, but enough to soften the ground. And the shoe on the left front hoof of Rip's horse had a big nick in it. Fargo was able to stay well back and follow the tracks, which were so plain that it didn't take a man of Fargo's skills to see them. A kid could have done it.

The trail led to the creek and turned into the trees not far from the marshy area where Paul Murray and the others who had died with him had been buried. Fargo wondered if Rip was going to try the same trick Angel had used when she was toying with Fargo, but the tracks never got within ten feet of the stream. Rip had gone into the trees for concealment, not because he thought he was being followed, but just so that nobody who happened to be out riding the countryside would see him by accident. He didn't think anyone was behind him. Why would he? He didn't know that Fargo was onto him.

He had left his house within fifteen minutes of Lem's visit. Fargo had given him a good lead and then gone after him. He was sure Rip would want to tell Murray of the big opportunity he was going to have.

There were two ways Murray could go when he heard the news. He could do as Lem had suggested to Rip and try to take over the farmhouses. Or he could go about setting up an ambush on the way to the cave, hoping to wipe out all the farmers at once. He hadn't had much luck against them so far when you thought about it, picking off one at a time. He was losing more men than he was killing. But now he'd have a chance to get the whole bunch of farmers in one place.

Or so he thought. Fargo had no intention of letting anything like that happen. He had a couple of ideas of his own. Either the farmers would set up their own ambush or they'd attack Murray where he was hiding, probably the latter. It would be a complete surprise, since Murray would think they had other plans.

After he'd ridden in the trees along the creek for several miles, Fargo saw that the tracks turned to leave the cover. He thought it was time to be careful, so he dismounted and looped the reins over a tree limb, preferring to travel on foot.

When he came to the edge of the trees, he saw a dilapidated building that rose up from the ground like something out of a crazy dream. It didn't look like any house that Fargo had ever seen. It was built up off the ground, unlike all the farmhouses Fargo had been in, and there was a skirting around it. It was three stories tall and had balconies on the second and third floors. There were lightning rods sticking up from all but one of the several cupolas that sat atop the third floor. The cupola that lacked a lightning rod had a weather vane that was bent over to one side.

Fargo had no idea how such a house had come to be there in the middle of nowhere. Some madman must have built it, he thought, a madman with a lot of money, but no one, mad or otherwise, had lived there for a long time. The house sagged to one side as if it were tired and about to lie down. The doors were missing.

But Murray was there. Fargo saw the gang's horses, and Rip's tracks led right up to it. The only guard was a man sitting on the porch that appeared to run all around the house. He was smoking a cigarette and not looking at anything in particular. It was plain that he didn't expect to be bothered.

Fargo faded back into the trees and walked to the Ovaro. It was time to get a little surprise ready for Murray. And for Rip, too.

"We'll go tonight," Fargo told the small group gathered in the front of Lem's house.

There were ten of them, the ones whose names Lem had called out to Rip and five others whom Fargo didn't know. The last five lived a bit farther away than the other farmers, but they had been at the wedding party, and they were just as eager to get rid of Murray as anybody else. Fargo thought ten might be enough. Although he had fifteen or sixteen men, Murray wouldn't be ready for any kind of attack. And his men hadn't shown themselves to be especially good fighters in any of the other encounters Fargo had seen them in. Besides, if the plan he had come up with worked out, Murray might not have fifteen men left when the fighting started, at least not able-bodied men.

"Murray's hiding at the Bigelow House," Lem told the group.

He had explained to Fargo earlier that the house had been built about twenty years earlier by a former sea captain from back east. The story was that he'd had a bad experience on his last voyage out and vowed to move as far from the sea as he could get.

"When he found this place, he figured he'd made it," Lem had explained. "You can't get much farther from the ocean than this."

But the sea captain hadn't had any better luck in his new house than he'd had on his final voyage. His wife got sick and died within the first year of their move. The captain himself had died of a fever not long afterward. His only child, a son about fifteen years old, had disappeared after the funeral and never been seen again. The only things that remained of the captain and his family were the house and some vague memories.

"Nobody ever wanted to live there after the captain died," Lem had told Fargo. "The house was like something you'd find in Maine, maybe, or someplace like that. Not here. Nobody who farms has time to take care of a house like that. And anyway the land wasn't fertile around there. Nobody knows why, but things just wouldn't grow. The house is just about falling down now, and nobody ever goes by there. Murray could stay there for a year, and nobody would ever know."

The people who were gathered at Lem's all knew where the Bigelow House was, though they never went near it. All of them also had ideas about what to do about Murray. And they all wanted to talk about them at once.

Lem quieted them down. "We're going to leave that up to Fargo. He's had more experience with men like Murray than we have."

There was a little mumbling, but it died down quickly as people realized the truth of what Lem was telling them.

"We'll leave here at about midnight," Fargo told them. "We'll stop on the way and get Rip. We'll have to take him with us to be sure he doesn't warn Murray."

"Why don't we just kill him?" Bob Tabor asked. "He's got enough of us killed, the son of a bitch."

"Why not give him a trial?" Fargo asked. "The sheriff might not want any part of this fight, but he'd have to keep Rip in his jail if you told him what's been going on. Then you could see to it that Rip gets a legal hanging."

There was some more mumbling and grumbling about that, but Lem calmed everybody down.

"Listen here," he said, "Fargo's got a plan about how to do this, and we don't have to kill Rip to do it. If we want to stay on the side of the law, such law as there is here, we ought to try not to hang people just for the hell of it. Rip's done us wrong, but he's still our neighbor. We ought to give him a chance to defend himself."

"I guess you're right about it," Cass Ellis said. "A man's got a right to have his side of the story heard before he gets hung."

"All right, then," Lem said. "Now let Fargo tell you what we're gong to do."

19

Rip didn't seem to know exactly what was going on. Which was just fine. Fargo didn't want him to know.

"I didn't think you'd show up here at this time of night," Rip said.

He was standing on his front porch again, holding the lantern he'd lit while he was still in the house. His hair was tousled, and he didn't look quite awake.

"I said morning," Lem told him. "It's past midnight, so it's morning. You better get ready to go. We'll help you."

Cass and Bob were already off their horses and walking toward Rip, who was going to be trussed up and tossed across a saddle for his trip. As the two men reached him, Rip's face changed. He seemed to know that something was wrong, and he turned back into his house.

Cass and Bob hesitated. They turned back and looked at Fargo as if to ask what to do next. In doing so, they gave Rip time to get to a gun.

The first shot came through the door and missed Cass by an inch or two. The second shot dropped Bob where he stood.

"Scatter," Fargo said. "I'll go around back."

By the time Fargo got to the back of the house, the door was already opening. Fargo let Rip get outside. Then he said, "Put the pistol down, Rip. You're not going anywhere."

Rip held up the lantern so that the light spread out some more. Fargo was still outside the circle of radiance.

"We know all about you and Murray," Fargo said.

"Then you're going to kill me anyway," Rip said.

"Nobody's going to kill you. We're just going to be sure you don't warn anybody."

"Bullshit," Rip said.

He fired a shot at Fargo, missed, and started to run around the house. Fargo didn't know where he was headed, but he knew he wasn't going to let him get there. He shot him twice.

The first shot knocked Rip off his stride and sent him stumbling toward his house. The second shot jerked him sideways, and he stumbled into the wall. When he hit it, his arm swung around and the lantern shattered on the wood. Coal oil spread out and started burning. Rip slid down to the ground.

"Who told you, Fargo?" he said. "How'd you know? Angel?"

"Nobody told. I just figured it out."

"Damn. Maybe you really are as smart as you think you are."

Rip slumped over to the side until his head was touching the ground. The pistol he'd been holding limply in his hand slipped from his fingers.

The wall of the house above him was dry, and the fire was spreading fast. Fargo rode back around to the front of the house. Bob Tabor was standing up, and Abby was tying something around his midsection.

"How's Bob?" Fargo asked of no one in particular.

Tabor answered for himself. "I'm just dandy. That bullet took a little fat off the side of my belly, but that's all right. I could stand to lose it. Hurts a little, but I can still ride. What about Rip?"

"He won't be doing any riding," Fargo said. "And I don't think we'll be able to save his house."

Everyone could see the flames now, and there was black smoke curling over the roof.

"Ain't worth it, anyhow," Cass said. "Funny, though. He was helping to run us off, and now it's his house that's going to burn."

"Let it go," Molly said. "It wasn't worth a damn. Are we going to talk all night, or are we going after Murray?"

"You know the answer to that," Lem said. "Let's ride."

Abby finished her bandaging, and Cass helped Tabor on his horse. When he was settled in the saddle, they rode away, leaving Rip's house in flames behind them.

* * *

It was quiet in the woods near the Bigelow House. The only sounds came from the trees when a squirrel woke up for a moment of chattering or from the soft whispers of the little group gathered there to take on the Murray gang.

There wasn't much of a moon, and the sky was cloudy, both of which made it hard to tell if there was more than one guard, or even if there was one. The house was quiet, and there was no movement anywhere near it. If there was a man on the porch, Fargo couldn't see him, but there was a dark shadow by the wall that could have been a man.

"If you get caught, we'll be in a mess," Lem said. "I'd feel better about it if you didn't have to cross all that open ground."

"It's the only way to get there," Fargo said. "If there's anybody on the porch, he's likely to be asleep. That's why we came at this time of the morning. Nobody's going to be awake in there. They all think they're as safe as if they were a thousand miles away."

"Well, you better get going then. If they're planning to set an ambush for us, they'll be getting up soon enough."

Fargo nodded and hefted the little keg of gunpowder that Molly had found in her barn. Talley had bought it to blast stumps with, but there weren't many stumps to blast. That meant there was a little bit of gunpowder left over.

"You be careful, Fargo," Molly said, leaning near his ear. "You don't want to blow off any important parts of yourself."

She nudged him with her elbow, and Fargo had to grin. He said, "Don't worry about me. If that house doesn't fall on me, I'll be just fine."

"You better get away long before it falls."

"I'll do my best. Just don't let anybody shoot me if I come running back this way."

Fargo waited until the moon was completely covered by clouds. Then he crouched as low as he could and set out toward the house. If somebody saw him, he was as good as dead, but he was counting on Murray to be lulled by the idea that the farmers were all waiting for morning to go to the cave on the river. He wouldn't have any idea what they really had planned for him, so he wouldn't have put out any extra guards.

Fargo judged it to be about a hundred yards to the house.

The ground was rough, and when he was about halfway there, he stumbled. He had to straighten up quickly and run awkwardly forward for a few steps to regain his balance, holding the gunpowder out in front of him like some kind of prize pig. When he was balanced again, he squatted quickly and waited to see if anybody had spotted him from the Bigelow House. The moon stayed behind the clouds, the house sat as still and quiet as ever, and after a couple of seconds Fargo moved on.

When he reached the house, he went straight to the back, looking for a break in the skirting so that he could slip underneath. He found one quickly enough and slithered through the opening. The smell of musk and raw earth filled his nose, and he bit back a sneeze as he wormed his way along.

When he figured he'd gone about far enough, he set the keg down and started squirming back out, unspooling the fuse as he went. The fuse wasn't as long as Fargo would have liked, but he thought it would do. He got almost back outside before it played out. He lit it and eased back out through the hole in the skirting.

As soon as he was out from under the house, he jumped up and started to run back toward the trees. He didn't worry about concealment this time. He didn't care who saw or heard him because by the time anybody tried to stop him, it was going to be too late for them to do much of anything.

Fargo was about twenty-five yards from the trees when the gunpowder went off with a muffled boom. Hearing the explosion, he hit the ground, slid forward a couple of feet, then swiveled around to see the results.

The house had already been leaning, and the blast finished it off. It exploded outward and upward. Boards flew through the air and landed all over, though none of them came very near to Fargo. What was left of the house toppled on over to the ground in a jagged pile.

By that time, Murray's men were running in six or eight directions, having no idea what had just happened. They'd been asleep and the house had exploded around them. They might have thought it was the end of the world, or they might have thought the house had been struck by a cannonball. Or maybe they were just running and not thinking at all.

Whatever the case may have been, they certainly weren't expecting the farmers to ride out of the trees and start shooting at them.

Most of Murray's men were the kind to sleep with their weapons right at hand, so they were armed, and they had the presence of mind to drop down to the ground and start shooting back. A few others made a mad dash for their horses, maybe in the hope that they could get away before they were killed. A couple just stood there, looking around as if they were dazed, and maybe they were. Those were the first to be cut down by the farmers' fire.

Fargo looked for Murray, but he didn't see him amid all the confusion. He did see Angel as she rode past him, looking neither to the right nor to the left. She was focused on someone, and Fargo knew it must be Murray. Scrambling to his feet, Fargo ran back into the trees to get his horse.

Within seconds he was aboard the Ovaro and riding in the direction Angel had gone. He rode right through the middle of the fighting and got a kaleidoscopic view of what was happening all around him.

To his left, Molly was off her horse and fighting hand to hand with two men, her hair wild as she smashed one of them to the ground with her right fist and grabbed the other around the neck with her free left hand. Abby was running toward the man that Molly was grappling with. She jumped on his back as Fargo passed on.

To the right, Lem was sitting on his horse and firing his pistol steadily. The flashes from its barrel were like red and orange streaks in the night. Tabor and Elliot were beside Lem, matching him shot for shot, and Murray's men, though they were firing back, were the ones getting the worst of it.

Then Fargo was through the crowd and alone, with Angel racing ahead of him and Murray in front of her.

After only a few more seconds, Murray turned back toward the trees, and his dark figure was soon lost in them. It was one thing to ride at speed across open ground. It was something else to do it among trees. In fact, it was impossible, and Fargo knew that Murray must have swerved into them because he had something in mind, maybe some trap he could spring on Angel. Fargo urged the Ovaro to go faster, hoping to reach Angel before she did anything foolish.

He was too late. She rode into the trees after her father.

It was dark in the trees, but they grew far enough apart for Fargo to maneuver the Ovaro through them. He could hear, but not see, Angel up ahead of him. Before she got to the creek, she turned aside, which meant that Murray was also sticking to the trees. Fargo didn't blame him. You couldn't ride fast, but you could ride, and there wasn't much danger of anybody shooting you with all the branches in the way. It didn't take much to turn a bullet aside.

Fargo drew the pistol he was wearing on the off chance that he'd get a shot at Murray. It wasn't his Colt, which had disappeared the night he fell from the horse and Murray had hauled him to the cave. But it was a good enough gun. He'd borrowed it from Molly, who was the only person around with more than one pistol. Farmers didn't generally go around armed. Fargo had shot the pistol a couple of times after borrowing it to get a feel for it, and it had done a good job against Rip. He thought it would do just as well when he had to use it on Murray.

He rode along for a minute or two, hoping to overtake Angel but not succeeding. Then up ahead he heard a horse whinny and someone screamed.

Angel.

Fargo couldn't go any faster. Limbs were already whipping him across the face, and he didn't want to damage his eyes. He hoped Murray hadn't killed Angel, but he wouldn't put it past him.

Before long, Fargo spotted Angel's horse standing calmly near a tree. Angel was lying on the ground. She wasn't moving. Fargo reined in the Ovaro and got down to see if she was just hurt or if she was dead.

She wasn't dead, and she wasn't hurt, except for some bruises. And she was angry.

"He waited for me," she told Fargo. "He hid behind that big tree over there and pulled back a limb. When I rode up, he let it go. It hit me square in the face and scared my horse, but I think I'm all right."

"At least he didn't try to kill you again," Fargo said. "Give him credit for that."

"He knew the horse would throw me. He thought I'd break my neck." Angel brushed leaves and dirt off her clothes, wincing only a little, and got back on her horse. "But it didn't work, and now I'm going to get him."

"He might be long gone by now."

"I don't think so. Where's he going to go?"

Fargo said he didn't know, but then he had an idea.

"He knows he's lost this fight. There won't be much left of his gang after those farmers get through with them tonight. He might be able to get another gang together, but it would take time, and the farmers would be a lot better organized before he could do it. He's either got to keep running or try to do something that will really hurt them."

"He won't run," Angel said. "How could he hurt them?"

Fargo didn't agree with her. He said, "I think he'll run. But I think he'll cause as much trouble as he can before he does. I think he might try to burn all the houses he can before we catch him."

"You're probably right. We have to stop him."

Fargo hoped they could. "We can try," he said.

20

They got out of the trees and rose as fast as they could. Fargo was sure that Murray had left the trees, too, and that he was well ahead of them.

"Where do you think he'll go first?" Angel said.

"Rip Johnson's house is closest," Fargo said. "He'll find out that we've done that job for him already, so he'll head for Lem's."

"We'll never get there before he burns the place."

"We might," Fargo said. "It's not as easy to burn a house as you think it is."

"Rip's place went up like a torch."

"That's because of the coal oil in the lantern. Murray doesn't have a lantern."

"How long do you think it'll take him to find one?"

"Not long," Fargo said.

When they reached the farm, Murray was nowhere to be seen, but his horse was outside the barn.

"He's in there," Angel said. "I'm going after him."

"I'll go," Fargo said. "You stay here."

Angel laughed as she slid off her horse. "Don't try to tell me what to do, Fargo. The only man who could was Pa, and I should never have listened to him in the first place."

Fargo shrugged and started toward the barn. Angel trailed along after him. They both stopped short of the big doors, which stood open. Fargo could hear someone inside, and he smelled coal oil. He realized that Murray was inside, splashing the coal oil around, getting ready to burn the barn first, and then the house.

"You in there, Murray?" he called.

The noise in the barn stopped. After a couple of seconds, Murray said, "Is that you, Fargo?"

"It's me," the Trailsman answered.

"Is Angel with you?"

"I'm here. Come on out, Pa. We can leave here and go somewhere else. Fargo won't try to stop us."

"How the hell can you say that?" Murray said. "The son of a bitch has blown up half my men, and I'm sure the other half are dead now. He'll kill me as soon as I show myself."

"No, he won't," Angel said. "I have a gun on him."

Fargo turned to see if Angel was trying to fool Murray, but she wasn't joking. She stood with her feet planted firmly, and in her right hand was a pistol aimed at Fargo's belt buckle.

"He's my pa," Angel said with a hint of apology. "When you get right down to it, I can't just let you kill him. And I don't want him to kill you, either."

Fargo was disgusted, not just with Angel but with himself. He should have known that blood ties mattered more than anything else to the Murrays. After all, hadn't Angel been with Murray when they'd dug up Paul's body and thrown Abby into the grave? Angel had changed since then, but she hadn't changed enough to want her father to die.

"You're not just leading me on, are you?" Murray asked from within the barn.

"Take a look," Angel said, her eyes on Fargo.

The Trailsman thought he could get in a shot or two if he went for his pistol, but the trouble with that was, Angel would get the first shot, and at that distance she wasn't likely to miss.

"You have him, all right," Murray said, and Fargo turned to see him peering around the opening into the barn. "How do I know it's not a trick?"

"It's not a trick," Angel said. "You can trust me, Pa."

"You betrayed me before, daughter. I can't ever trust you again, not after that."

"I didn't do anything to hurt you. I just didn't want you to kill people who'd helped me without giving them a chance to fight back."

"One thing you should have learned from me," Murray said, "is that you never give anybody a fair chance. Fargo

149

could tell you that. He blew up that house without a warning. Isn't that right, Fargo."

"Nobody was killed when the house blew up," Fargo said. "After that, everybody had a chance to get away. You managed it."

"That's because I'm a little smarter than most of the men I surrounded myself with. I could have used somebody like you, Fargo, but you're a little too delicate for the job."

"If you mean I'm not a killer, you're right, Murray."

"I don't think my daughter is, either, but I'm going to give her a chance to prove herself once and for all. I'll come out of the barn, Angel, if you'll kill Fargo. Right now. Pull the trigger."

"I can't do that," Angel said.

"That's what I was afraid of," Murray said. "So I'll have to do it myself."

He stepped into the opening, and when he did Fargo dived to the side. The sound of a pistol blast echoed from the barn as Fargo rolled over and came up shooting. His bullet knocked a chunk out of the side of the doorway, but Murray had already ducked back inside. Fargo turned his head to see Angel on her knees. She had dropped her pistol and was holding both hands to her stomach.

"He . . . shot me," she said.

"He was shooting at me," Fargo told her. "But I moved."

"I think . . . he meant to do it."

"No," Fargo said, though he wasn't entirely sure.

It didn't matter. He didn't think Angel heard him.

She folded in the middle and fell forward so that her forehead was touching the ground. She stayed like that without moving, and Fargo knew she was dead.

"You killed your daughter, Murray," he called into the barn. "And now I'm coming for you."

"Come ahead, Fargo," Murray yelled back.

Fargo got to his feet and walked to the side so that Murray couldn't see him from the barn door. When he reached the barn, he turned his back to the wall and walked to the door with his shoulders rubbing against the rough wood. The pistol he had borrowed from Molly was in his hand.

"Come inside, Fargo," Murray said.

Fargo didn't reply.

"You killed my son," Murray said after a few seconds of silence, "and now you've killed my daughter. Why don't you face me like a man?"

"I didn't kill anybody, Murray," Fargo told him, thinking that Murray would go to his death blaming someone else for all his troubles. "If you hadn't raided the wedding party, your son would still be alive. And you're the one who shot your daughter, not me."

"You jumped out of the way. I was trying to kill you, not her."

"Maybe you believe that, but I don't. You already tried to kill her once. This time, you did it."

"I never tried to kill her. She just needed to be taught a lesson. You don't betray your family."

"What do you call it when you kill them?" Fargo asked.

There was a long silence. Fargo waited it out.

"Are you still out there, Fargo?" Murray asked.

Again, Fargo didn't answer.

"What are you waiting for? Do you think those farmers are going to come back and help you? I hope they do come back, Fargo. Because if they do, I'll pick them off from the loft, one at a time. I'll start with Abby Watkins. You watched my daughter die, and you can watch the Watkins bitch die, too."

Murray's voice sounded different. He'd moved farther back in the barn, or so it seemed, probably headed for the loft. Fargo thought he might be able to catch him before he got there, so he stepped around the wall and into the barn. There was the sharp smell of coal oil mingled with the smell of hay and manure.

Murray was already at the top of the ladder to the loft, and he jumped forward just as Fargo fired at him. The bullet knocked off the heel of Murray's boot, but Murray rolled away, unhurt.

"That was close, Fargo," he said. "If you'd been more of a man, you'd have come in and faced me. Maybe you could have killed me. As it stands now, you'll never get me."

It was dark in the barn, but it didn't matter. Murray was out of sight in the loft anyhow.

But he wasn't as safe as he thought he was. He couldn't see Fargo any better than Fargo could see him, and the flooring of the loft was just planking that wouldn't stop a bullet. Fargo crossed the barn until he was standing under the flooring.

"You still up there, Murray?" he shouted.

"Right here," Murray answered, and Fargo fired at the sound.

The bullet when through the planking, and dust drifted down on Fargo.

"You missed, Fargo, but I thought you'd come over here and try that. I was hoping you would. Welcome to hell."

Fargo saw something falling from the loft. A lit match. It fell lazily toward a stack of hay near the wall.

When the match hit the hay, it ignited the coal oil that Murray had splashed on it. The hay blazed up quickly, and smoke poured out of the stack.

Fargo heard footsteps pounding on the floor above him. He didn't try a shot. It wouldn't have been worth it. He moved out from under the floor. The heat from the fire was already scorching him.

Murray's dark figure appeared at the edge of the loft floor at the side of the barn opposite the fire. Fargo took a shot just as Murray jumped.

The shot went past Murray's head, and Murray landed on another stack of hay. He rolled down the side of it, flinging hay and dust all around him. When he hit the ground, he rolled under a wagon and took a shot at where Fargo had been standing, but Fargo was no longer there.

The fire was spreading rapidly, and the Trailsman knew that the barn was lost. He also knew that if he stayed inside, he would be burned alive. Or dead, if Murray shot him. He preferred to leave Murray there to burn instead, so he headed for the doorway.

By the time he got there, the fire had already gone up the side of the wall, engulfing most of it. The floor of the loft had caught, and it wouldn't be long before the roof was afire as well. Fargo didn't believe Murray had a chance.

Murray felt differently.

As he reached the doorway, Fargo heard something over the crackling of the flames. He turned to see the wagon bearing down on him. Murray was behind it, pushing, but with nothing to guide it in the front, it didn't go straight for the door. It veered to one side and headed for the wall, exposing Murray, who jumped to get behind it again.

Fargo had only a couple of shots left, and he wanted to make them count. He stepped back into the barn, which was rapidly becoming an inferno, and looked for Murray.

The smoke was thick and stung Fargo's eyes. He took shallow breaths. After a couple of seconds, he saw Murray standing to his right. In the light of the flames, Murray looked like some kind of demon. He had his back to the burning wall, and his pistol was in his hand. He was about to pull the trigger, but Fargo didn't give him a chance.

Fargo fired one shot, and the pistol jerked from Murray's hand and flipped backward. Murray looked down at his hand in wonderment, then looked back at Fargo.

"That was a lucky shot, Fargo. Now I don't have a gun." Murray had to stop and cough for a second. The smoke was getting to him. "But I don't need one. You're a man of honor, Fargo, and you wouldn't shoot an unarmed man. I know that, and so do you."

"I have one bullet left," Fargo said. "Just how sure are you that I won't use it on you?"

He took a step forward, pointing his pistol at Murray's head.

"I'm sure," Murray said. "Men like you will kill in an even fight, but you'd never take an unfair advantage. I'm going to walk right out of here."

"Jed Brand was a good friend of mine," Fargo said. "You didn't kill him, but you caused his death. You caused plenty of misery and death before he died and more since. No one would blame me if I shot you."

Fargo took another determined step forward, and Murray took another back. The fire must have been blistering his back, Fargo thought.

"But you won't." Murray coughed. "I know you won't."

Murray had been splashing coal oil all around the barn. There was no way he could have avoided getting some of it on him, Fargo thought, and he was right. As Murray started to take a step forward, his clothing suddenly ignited. Sometimes you just had to let a man bring about his own destruction.

"No," Fargo said, "I won't shoot you. But you might wish I would."

In an instant Murray was enveloped in flames. His clothing burned. His beard and hair were afire. He screamed and ran toward Fargo, who stepped aside and let him go. Murray had dropped his pistol. Fargo thought he recognized it and picked it up. It was hot to the touch, but Fargo didn't drop it. It was his own Colt. Murray knew a good weapon when he stole it. Fargo put it in his holster and continued to hold Molly's gun in his hand as he went out of the barn.

Murray was rolling on the ground, still screaming. He could roll for a long time, Fargo thought, without putting out the fire.

"Shoot me!" Murray screamed. "For God's sake, Fargo!"

"I wouldn't shoot an unarmed man," Fargo told him. "You said so yourself."

Murray continued to scream, but Fargo could no longer make out the words. The Trailsman walked over to Angel, lifted her up, and carried her into the house.

21

It was a little after first daylight when Lem, Abby, and Molly came riding up. There was nothing left of Lem's barn but a pile of ashes and blackened timbers. A smaller pile of charred debris remained not far away, but nobody noticed it.

"Good God a'mighty, Fargo," Lem said, wrinkling his nose at the smell of the burned barn and of something else that was harder to identify. "What happened here?"

Fargo gave them a short account of the fight with Murray.

"That's him over there," Fargo said, pointing to the burned carcass.

"I thought I smelled something funny," Lem said.

"Doesn't look like much now, does he?" Molly said. "Hard to believe he had us all running scared for so long. Well, we won't be running now."

"He still managed to cause a hell of a mess of trouble," Lem said. "No matter how he looks and smells now. And he finally got to my place, too."

"He got your barn," Fargo said, "but he didn't get your house. And he didn't get anybody else's house. Not today."

"We can build a new barn," Abby said. "It's just a building. Where's Angel?"

Fargo told them about that, too.

"She's inside," he added. "I laid her on the table."

"I'd be proud to sit up with her," Lem said.

"So would I, I think," Abby said. "Even if she did try to bury me alive, she wasn't all bad."

"She wasn't all good, either," Molly said, "but even at that she didn't deserve the kind of family she had."

"What about you?" Fargo asked them. "How did things turn out at the Bigelow House?"

"We got all the bastards," Lem said. "Some of them are just wounded, but we left them to take care of each other. If they do, that's fine. They won't be bothering anybody for a while. And if they don't, well, to hell with them. We gave them every chance."

"Jed would be glad to know you settled everything for him," Abby told Fargo. "I knew you could do it."

There'd been times when Fargo hadn't shared her confidence, but he figured he'd done what Jed would have wanted. And he'd done what he wanted. He couldn't let his friend be murdered and just walk away.

"I guess you'll be leaving now," Molly said.

She was right. Fargo didn't have anything to tie him to the farmers now.

"I'll head out tomorrow," he said. "After Angel's funeral."

"And you're sure there's no way we could make a farmer of you?" Molly asked.

Abby looked at her suspiciously and asked, "Have you been thinking about farming, Fargo?"

"Not a whole lot," Fargo said. "I've been thinking more about mountains with snow on the tops, and some country where there aren't a lot of farms all jammed up together."

Lem laughed. "I wouldn't say we're all jammed together here, Fargo. Plenty of room for another farm. Lots more of them, to tell the truth."

"It may look that way to you. Not to me, though."

"Well," Molly said, getting another suspicious look from Abby, "if you're ever back this way, Fargo, stop in and visit for a while."

Fargo never knew where he might be the next week or the next month, but he knew how way led on to way, and he didn't think he'd ever find himself in this part of the country again, at least not for a long time.

"I'll be sure and do that," he said.

LOOKING FORWARD!

**The following is the opening
section of the next novel in the exciting
Trailsman series from Signet:**

THE TRAILSMAN #261
Desert Death Trap

*Nevada Territory, Summer 1861—
Deceit, danger, and death at every turn.*

Over a low rise to the east appeared a young maiden, running as if her life depended on it. Long raven hair streamed behind her as she swiftly descended a game trail. She moved with the natural grace of an antelope, a comparison heightened by the buckskin dress that clung to her lithe form.

Skye Fargo was about to saddle up after a good night's sleep when he spotted her. He watched with keen interest, enticed by the flash of her shapely legs. She was so intent on running, she didn't spot his camp, hidden in the brush less than a stone's throw from the bottom of the rise.

The reason for her flight became plain when three men sprinted over the top of the hill.

Fargo's lake-blue eyes narrowed. The trio were also on foot, which in itself was remarkable. No one in their right mind tried to cross the high desert country between the Great Salt Lake and the Cascades without a horse. Even more peculiar was that one of her pursuers was white, the other red, and the third black. "What the hell?" he wondered aloud.

The white pursuer wore just about the silliest outfit Fargo ever saw, a two-piece affair that resembled bright red longjohns. Bushy sideburns and a thick mustache framed his pale face. His gait was as odd as his appearance; he loped in long, stiff-legged motion, attended by the windmill pumping of broomstick arms.

Next was a husky Indian more sensibly attired in a breechclout and knee-high moccasins. Fargo couldn't be completely sure at that distance, but it sure looked to him that the warrior was an Apache. Which was preposterous—Apache territory was many leagues to the south.

Last came the black man. A strapping specimen, he had on a pair of faded jeans and a floppy brown hat that hid half his ruggedly chiseled face. He didn't seem to be exerting himself all that hard yet he had no trouble keeping up with the others.

The maiden looked back, saw them, and ran faster.

Fargo didn't know what was going on, but he wasn't about to stand there and let the men catch her. Experience told him they had to be up to no good. The maiden dashed past his camp without a sideways glance. Dropping his bedroll, Fargo turned toward his horse. The Ovaro was twenty yards away, slaking its thirst at a small spring. He intended to mount up but a quick look showed the three men were already near the bottom of the rise.

Impulsively, Fargo hurtled from the scrub brush. He thought it would be easy to intercept the three before they overtook their quarry. But he gave them too little credit. Once on flat ground, they had doubled their speed.

Fargo was in excellent condition, his sinews hardened to iron by a life in the wild, his stamina second to none. He settled into a long stride, the jangle of his spurs a constant reminder that he might have been better off using the Ovaro.

It pushed Fargo to his limit but bit by bit he narrowed

the gap. Soon he was only thirty yards behind. Then twenty. Then ten. He could see beads of sweat on the back of the black's neck when, alerted by the sound of his spurs, the man suddenly glanced over a shoulder. Seconds later the Apache did the same. Last to hear, the gaudily garbed white man twisted around.

"Hold it right there!" Fargo bellowed. He was almost on top of them and about to palm his Colt when he realized, to his considerable amazement, all three were unarmed. But they were far from defenseless. The black man whirled and cocked a fist the size of a sledgehammer. Only Fargo's razor-sharp reflexes spared him from having his jaw broken.

"Mr. Samuels, no!" the white man bawled, but the big black man paid no mind.

Fargo dodged a second blow, and a third. He landed a solid jab to the gut that would usually double a man over, but Samuels merely grunted. Whirling to dodge a flurry of jabs, he glimpsed the Apache, standing aloof. The white's mouth was agape. At least they weren't lending a hand.

Samuels was nothing if not determined. He waded in again, his fists flying.

It as all Fargo could do to keep from having his head knocked off. He blocked, ducked, then delivered an upper-cut that jarred the bigger man onto his heels. In the blink of an eye Fargo had his Colt out and leveled. "Enough!" he barked, thumbing back the hammer. "Simmer down or you'll eat lead."

Undaunted, Samuels raised his arms again but the jasper in the red longjohns grabbed his wrist.

"Be sensible, my good fellow! Let's get to the bottom of this before you resume pummeling him." He had a British accent as thick as jam. To Fargo he said, "I demand to know the meaning of this unjustified assault, sir."

"Unjustified?" Fargo replied.

"What else would you call it?" Samuels angrily growled. "You had no call to come rushin' up on us like you did."

Fargo nodded at the maiden, who had stopped and turned about sixty feet ahead. "We'll let the girl you were after be the judge of that." He beckoned, and after a few seconds of hesitation she jogged toward them.

"Do you know Morning Star?" the Englishman inquired. "Is this some unfathomable lark on her part?"

The Apache had folded his muscular arms across his broad chest and showed no inclination to join in the talk.

Samuels, though, shook a calloused fist. "If this throws us off the pace, I'll report you to the officials! And take it out of your hide, to boot."

Fargo never like being threatened. "You're welcome to try."

"You talk mighty big when you're holdin' a six-shooter," the black man snapped. "Why don't you holster it and we'll see just how tough you really are."

"Now, now, Mr. Samuels," the Englishman cautioned. "Violence is the last resort of the feebleminded."

"Are you callin' me stupid? Just because you're some high-falutin' lord muck-a-muck doesn't give you the right to insult folks."

"I am an earl, not a lord," the Englishman curtly replied. "I wish you would bother to remember that." Facing Fargo, he gave a slight bow. "Earl Desmond Sherwood, at your service. I trust you will overlook Mr. Samuels's tantrum. He has them with distressing frequency."

Samuels opened his mouth to say something but fell silent at the arrival of the gorgeous maiden with the lustrous black hair. She also had an effect on Sherwood and the Apache. The former drew himself up to his full height and smoothed his thin patch of russet hair. The latter ran his gaze up and down her shapely figure like a hungry man who craved a feast.

Fargo touched his hat brim. Up close he could tell she was a Crow, which was as strange as everything else. The Crows lived a week's ride or better to the east. "Do you savvy English?"

"I speak your tongue quite well, thank you," Morning Star said, her enunciation superb. "Why did you attack these men?"

"I saw they were after you and figured I'd lend a hand." Fargo drank in the beauty of her smooth complexion, dazzling dark eyes, and teeth as white as the purest snow.

"You thought they meant to harm me?" Morning Star

regarded him with heightened interest. "That was noble of you. But your help was not needed. They pose no threat. They would not risk being disqualified."

"Hear that, did you, mister?" Samuels rasped. "You made a jackass of yourself for nothing. We're practicing, is all."

Thoroughly confused, Fargo lowered his Colt. "For what?"

Desmond Sherwood took it on himself to answer. "Why, the great race, of course. The First Annual Nugget Chamber of Commerce Test of Endurance in the Art of Footracing. With a grand prize of ten thousand dollars."

A couple of years ago a rich vein of silver had been discovered down near the California border, and ever since prospectors and others hoping to get rich quick had been scouring the mountains and deserts for more. Whenever a new strike was made, a new settlement immediately sprang up. Nugget, as Fargo recollected hearing, was one of the latest in a long string.

"They've been vigorously promoting the event for four or five months now," Sherwood related.

This was the first Fargo had heard of it. He twirled the Colt into his holster. "My mistake."

"And that's it?" Samuels prodded. "You pull a damned hogleg on us and expect there won't be any hard feelings."

"Forgive and forget, what?" Desmond Sherwood said. "It was a simple misunderstanding. I'm satisfied." He smiled at Fargo. "Perhaps you should give some thought to attending the festivities. Head due east and you can't miss the town." Squinting up at the sun, he declared, "We're wasting valuable training time, lady and gentlemen. Shall we press on?"

And just like that, the four of them resumed running, Morning Star once again in the lead. As they departed Fargo noticed the most remarkable fact of all. Even though the ground was littered with countless stones that could cut flesh to ribbons, she was barefoot.

Fargo turned and hiked back to the spring. The notion of paying Nugget a visit appealed to him. He had been on the go for over a week, traveling from San Francisco to

Cheyenne. A day or two of cards, whiskey and women, not necessarily in that order, were just what he needed.

By the middle of the morning the temperature had climbed into the nineties. Fargo pulled his hat brim low against the harsh glare of the sun and held the pinto to a walk. The air landscape baked under the sun's onslaught, fit for lizards, snakes and scorpions, and little else.

Fargo shifted in the saddle. Morning Star and the others had long since vanished into the haze. He shook his head and clucked to the Ovaro. Anyone who went running around in that heat had to be loco, ten thousand dollars or not. He wouldn't do it for twice that much.

Their tracks were as plain as the buckle on Fargo's belt. All he had to do was backtrack to their starting point. What he found was yet another surprise in a day chock full of them so far.

Nugget was no sleepy mining camp. It had buildings and hitch rails and water troughs, its streets crowded even in the heat of day. Banners had been strung, and somewhere a piano was playing.

A festive air held sway. Everyone Fargo passed on his way in either smiled or cheerfully bid him welcome. As he drew rein and started to slide down, a portly man in a suit and bowler barreled toward him with a pudgy hand thrust out.

"Greetings, stranger! Welcome to our grand celebration. I'm Mayor Jonathan Quinby." The mayor had the grip of a soggy sponge.

"What is it you're celebrating, exactly?" Fargo asked. "The footrace?"

"Heard about that, did you?" Quinby hooked his thumbs in his vest. "But the race is only a small part of the overall proceedings." He had droopy jowls that quivered as he spoke, and cheeks worthy of a chipmunk. "I take it you haven't kept up with news, then?"

"I've been on the trail awhile."

"Ah. Well, surely you've heard about the creation of the Nevada Territory? Not that long ago President Lincoln appointed a territorial governor. And Nugget has been officially recognized as a town." Mayor Quinby puffed out his chest like a rooster about to crow. "We're celebrating with two full weeks of frolic and fun. The footrace is the highlight but by no means the only activity planned."

Fargo scanned the streaming currents of contented humanity. "Everyone sure seems to be having a good time."

"And so should you, my friend, so should you!" Quinby always talked as if he were on the stump. "Many of our businesses are offering discount rates for the duration, and there's free beer every evening from five until five-thirty courtesy of the chamber of commerce."

"Your town will go broke before this is over."

"I beg to differ, sir," Quinby said earnestly. "Our coffers are swollen with revenue from the silver mines. Why, how else do you suppose we can afford a cash prize of ten thousand dollars to the winner of the footrace and two thousand to whoever comes in second?" He puffed out his chest even more. "It was my brainstorm, I'm proud to say. Races are all the rage in places like Denver and St. Louis. And there's one down New Mexico way that annually draws thousands of spectators."

Fargo had witnessed the New Mexico race a few years ago, and he agreed it was a crowd pleaser.

"Perhaps you would care to enter?"

"Me?" Fargo chuckled. "That'll be the day."

"Why not? The entry fee is only a dollar. And you certainly look fit enough. I daresay you might give the favorites a run for their money." Quinby laughed at his little witticism.

"How many are running?"

"Fifty-seven. We hope to have sixty by race time the day after tomorrow. You can register at the Quinby Hotel or—"

"You own the hotel?"

"Just one of them. And one of the banks. And several other businesses. It's safe to say no one has more clout in Nugget than I do. If I can be of any help to you in any regard, you have only to ask." Doffing his bowler, Nugget's leading citizen scampered off to greet someone else.

Fargo spied a group of ten or eleven Crows across the street. Relatives and friends of Morning Star, he reckoned.

He decided to stretch his legs. There was the usual assortment of townspeople, prospectors, miners and gamblers, plus more than a few curly wolves. Hardened gunmen and the like, hovering like hawks looking for something to kill.

Although it wasn't yet noon the saloons were open and doing a brisk business. Fargo pushed through batwing doors and shouldered through the noisy crowd to the bar. He paid for a bottle of whiskey, then searched in vain for an empty table. Venturing back out, he sat on a bench in the shade of the overhang, tipped the booze to his mouth and let it sear his insides. It was the real article, not the watered down excuse for coffin varnish some establishments served. Fargo smacked his lips in appreciation. About to take another swallow, he paused.

Two Apaches were coming up the boardwalk. Mimbres, unless he was mistaken, the same as the Apache runner he had encountered. They wore headbands, long-sleeved shirts and pants, over which they wore breechclouts—an Apache custom, as were their knee-high moccasins. One cradled a rifle, the other had a bow and quiver slung across his back. Both had big bone-handled knives on their hips.

Fargo had nothing against Apaches, nor against any other tribe, for that matter. He had lived with various Indians from time to time, and learned that just like whites, there were good ones and bad ones.

Pedestrians gave the duo a wide berth. No outright hostility was shown, just a wariness born of instinct. The warriors were like wolves among sheep, and the sheep knew it. Most of them, anyway. For as Fargo looked on, four toughs who had been lounging against the saloon straightened and planted themselves in the path of the Apaches.

"Lookee here!" declared a scrawny excuse for a gunman whose Remington had notches on the grips. "More mangy Injuns! It's gettin' so a fella can't hardly turn around without trippin' over one."

"They're worse than lice, Mitch," commented a man with straw-colored hair. "What say we squish 'em just for the hell of it?"

A third hitched at his gunbelt. "Count me in, Harley.

The only thing I like more than stompin' redskins is spittin' on their graves."

The Appaches had halted and were waiting for the whites to move out of their way. Their faces betrayed neither fear nor worry.

Mitch spread his legs and placed his hands on his hips. "How about it, you red devils? Care to oblige me and my pards? We'll buck you out so fast, your heads will spin."

"Look at 'em!" Harley scoffed. "Standing there like bumps on a log. Hell, I bet they don't understand a lick of English." He poked the foremost warrior. "Come on! What does it take to rile you lunkheads?"

Passersby were stopping to stare. An elderly rider reined up and leaned on his saddle horn. No one seemed particularly eager to intervene.

Mitch drew his Remington and performed a fancy spin. "See this, redskins? I've got ten dollars that says I can draw and blow out your wicks before you so much as lift a finger."

Harley laughed and poked the foremost warrior a second time. Again, neither Apache reacted. They might as well be sculpted from marble.

Fargo took another swig of whiskey. The goings-on had nothing to do with him. He was better off sitting there and minding his own business. Butting in would only land him in trouble he didn't need. So why, then, did he hear himself say, "They're not bothering anyone. Let them be."

All four gunnies turned. Mitch and Harley swapped glances and sauntered toward him, side by side.

"What do we have here?" Mitch asked no one in particular.

"One of those good Samaritans the Bible-thumpers are always gabbin' about." Harley snickered. "How about if we show him what we think of his kind around these parts?"

Fargo treated himself to another long swallow, wiped his mouth with a sleeve, and commented without looking up, "Go play in the street before I forget how green you are."

Harley bristled like a riled porcupine. "Mister, you're about to lose half your teeth." He hiked up his boot to kick.

"You first," Fargo rejoined, and came up off the bench swifter than a striking rattler.

No other series has this much historical action!

THE TRAILSMAN

To order call: 1-800-788-6262

Ralph
Cotton

"Gun-smoked, blood-stained, gritty believability...
Ralph Cotton writes the sort of story we all hope
to find within us." —Terry Johnston

"Authentic Old West detail." —*Wild West Magazine*

JURISDICTION   20547-2
Young Arizona Ranger Sam Burrack has vowed to bring
down a posse of murderous outlaws—and save the
impressionable young boy they've befriended.

DEVIL'S DUE   20394-1
The second book in Cotton's "Dead or Alive" series. The
Los Pistoleros gang were the most vicious outlaws
around—but Hart and Roth thought they had them under
control...Until the jailbreak.

Also Available:
BORDER DOGS   19815-8
BLOOD MONEY   20676-2
BLOOD ROCK   20256-2

Available wherever books are sold, or
to order call: 1-800-788-6262